BULLET POOF

A Pedro the Water Dog Saves the Planet Primer

AVIS KALFSBEEK

Let's Keep in Touch

Find more stories, updates, and community at

www.AvisKalfsbeek.com

Peace is Here podcast:

Email: aviskalfsbeek@gmail.com

Facebook: @aviskalfsbeekauthor

Instagram: @pedrothewaterdog @avis_kalfsbeek

Patreon: patreon.com/aviskalfsbeek

Substack: https://substack.com/@aviskalfsbeek

Peace and love.

Acknowledgements:

Benjamin Katz Creative, RAWtools / Guns to Gardens Network, Handmade Moments

My deep respect goes to the D-I-Y (punk) philosophers and real-life bicycle builders

whose craft inspires the peaceful ride.

The imaginary bicycles in the chapter headings carry a number: the guns erased to build

it. Research supports the assumption that one surrendered assault rifle yields roughly 3.3

pounds of reclaimable steel, and that each bicycle frame is made from approximately 75

percent gun steel by weight.

'

ISBN 978-1-953965-16-5 (Hardback)

ISBN 978-1-953965-17-2 (Paperback)

ISBN 978-1-953965-18-9 (Ebook)

www.AvisKalfsbeek.com

For my godson Henry Hiram Kalfsbeek

For the people working every day to reduce weapons

For my uncle James Kalfsbeek and my father Peter Kalfsbeek, who in the late 1960s started a company to lock gun barrels. At a conference in Montreal in 1970, they displayed a large poster of my three-year-old brother and cousin with the words: "Protect Your Loved Ones."

In 1970, Americans owned an estimated 90 to 100 million firearms, largely tied to hunting culture. By 2025, civilian-owned firearms have risen to nearly 400 million, even as fewer households own guns overall.

Because there is a dog in the story

The following pages dive into gun culture with an occasional bad word at the level equivalent to a PG-13 rating in film.

Dear Reader,

Pedro worried about the guns. He asked if the topic was too much for a story about bikes, hikes, and best friends. I wondered too.

While this book does not feature graphic violence, it deals with the reality of what happens when a weapon is present. There is a scene involving the wounding of an animal. If that is a journey you aren't ready to take, I understand. But if you trust me to carry you toward hope, let's press on.

This story is fiction, but the grief it touches is not. Within a few miles of my home, I have seen the sorrow a gun brings.

Gun statistics are staggering.

At the end of the book, you will find a list of the specific firearms used in American mass shootings, not to glorify them, but to name them. Naming them helps disarm their legacy. Read it if you are ready.

You will hear from Pedro at the end of this book. He stays safe in this story.

Thank you for riding alongside us.

Avis Kalfsbeek

One Hundred Twelve Million Bicycles

23,000,000 military-style semiautomatic rifles,

155,000,000 other rifles and shotguns, and

145,000,000 handguns are in U.S. civilian hands.[1]

112,000,000 Americans rode a bicycle last year.[2]

CHAPTER 1

Sandglass Standard: Measuring the future by the path, not the clock

23.6 LBS. – 5.4 GUNS ERASED

Tilly and Camas pound the Lake Bijou Nez trail, their jogger strollers a blur of motion under jagged alpine peaks. Inside the strollers, in a modern time when many say the world will fail to sustain human life, their toddlers are tucked under baseball caps.

Aquene, Tilly's little carrot-top, clutches a zucchini stick like a tiny Olympic torch.

"Are we training for a marathon I didn't sign up for?" Camas calls, winded. Her strawberry-blonde hair curls around her beanie. She wears neon running gear and grips her stroller handle like a white-water kayak oar.

"We agreed babies wouldn't mean inertia." Tilly, lean and olive-skinned with a cascade of dark hair, maintains her stride.

"How many more miles of penance do we owe for those fries?"

Camas calls.

"Your body's a temple. I'm helping with the renovations."

"Damn the truffle butter," Camas says.

Aquene launches a half-mashed rice cracker from her stroller. It arcs through the air, a miniature projectile. Pedro, Tilly's black, curly-haired water dog, bounds forward and snatches it mid-air.

"Nice catch, P!" Tilly says.

In the other seat, Eland erupts in giggles. He reaches out and grabs Pedro's tail. The stroller swerves.

"Eland, no! We run on our own watts, buddy." Camas stops and unwraps her son's hand from the dog's fur. Pedro licks Eland's face.

Tilly laughs. "He loves P."

"He loves everyone and everything. He's my Zen master in a diaper."

"We're basically raising little versions of each other. Aquene's a red-haired mystery."

"I talked to her every day in your belly. She popped out ginger."

Their feet fall into rhythm.

A sharp crack splits the air.

Tilly slams on her brakes. Camas veers sharply.

"Boom!" Aquene claps.

"WTF?" Camas blurts.

"That wasn't a truck backfire," Tilly says, looking across the lake.

"Nope." Camas pulls out her phone. "Probably that damn Liberty Lead Institute. They aren't supposed to be firing this early."

They roll the strollers over the wooden planks of the dock toward Ike's weathered houseboat. Ike, leather-skinned with a white beard, is hunched over a propane stove.

"Hey, Ike!" Tilly calls. "Can you watch the munchkins while we paddle?"

He moves a pot, turns the gas off, and steps to the edge of the boat.

"There was a shooting in Spokane. An elementary school. Dawn Redwood."

The wind picks up, chilling the sweat on Tilly's neck.

"Twenty-eight kids," Ike whispers. "They're saying it's one of the worst."

Camas kneels by Eland's stroller.

Tilly's hand finds the curls on Pedro's head. She squeezes. "That's Brock Highside's school."

"Your rafting friend?" Camas asks.

Tilly nods. She turns to Ike. "We heard a shot a few minutes ago."

"Liberty Lead," Ike says. "They got a permit for a range and a security school. Couldn't even pause this morning."

"Proppin' it up Heston style," Camas says. She pulls two small life jackets from the stroller.

Aquene points a chubby finger. "Pirate!"

Ike looks up, a weak smile crossing his face. He picks up his ukulele. "Of course I'll watch these hummus-breathed scallywags. We'll swab the deck and arrange a parley."

"Chiver teember!" Aquene shouts.

"Shiver me timbers," Ike laughs as he takes her from Tilly over the side of the boat.

Tilly and Camas stand tall on their paddleboards, gliding across the glassy lake. Pedro sits at the front of Tilly's board, ears up.

"How's the no drinking going?" Tilly asks. Her paddle slices the water.

Camas watches the ripples fan out from her board. "A day like today makes you want to. But I won't."

Tilly nods. "I saw Dust downtown the other day. Open carry."

"Dust? The one from kindergarten?"

CHAPTER 2

Eland's Wish: Safety and joy for the next generation

14.2 LBS. – 2.8 GUNS ERASED

Hand-painted murals of stars and beets cover the wooden out-buildings at Sandglass Meadows School. Goats and a miniature cow chew methodically by the gate. A weathered barn sign reads: *Teaching peace, one heart at a time.*

Barnaby, a white alpaca, snorts.

Tilly and Camas roll the strollers through the gate. Pedro follows, tail wagging. Aquene wears a blue felt crown and second-hand rain boots. Eland holds a bag of goat treats as if it is full of gold.

Parents drop off children in handwoven slings and homemade carts. One mom hums a bluegrass lullaby. Camas gives her a thumbs up.

On the schoolhouse porch, Hollis Truemilk, the headmaster, lifts a tiny bell. His gray braid sways as he raises his arms like a conductor.

"Let the day unfold like dandelion fluff," he says. "Let bodies be strong, minds be kind, and hearts be unarmored."

"Unarmored, huh?" Camas says. "Might need to check if that goat got the memo."

"And Dawn Redwood Elementary," Tilly says softly.

The goat headbutts a post.

Miss Larklyn kneels on the wool rug. The air smells of cedar and beeswax. Her hair is braided with ribbons; her blouse is the color of chamomile tea. She smiles as the starlings arrive, boots thumping on the wood floor.

"Today we'll make leaf boats for the stream and read about the peaceful prairie," she says. "But first, let's greet our animal friends."

The children gather near the barnyard gate to meet the school's rescued residents: a sheep named Cumulus, two goats, Brother Hops the rabbit, an alpaca, and the meditative cow. Miss Larklyn leads a chant about coexistence. A boy named Milo hands the goat a leaf.

Tilly lingers at the fence. "This place is a little surreal," she whispers. "I keep expecting hobbits to walk out of the garden shed."

"I know," Camas says. "Or livestock union negotiations."

"I'd vote with the cow," Tilly says.

They sit on a sun-warmed log beside the pen.

Camas watches Eland pet the cow's nose. "Feels like another planet here," Camas says. "A slow, mossy planet where hugs have bylaws."

"It's perfect."

Pedro curls up at their feet.

Hollis Truemilk walks past the parent circle. He leans in to whisper. "A parent gathering is Thursday morning in the Garden Room. We discuss our approach to emergencies. No mention around the children."

Tilly nods. Camas glances toward the tree line beyond the fence.

"Why do I feel like the real world starts the second we leave this parking lot?" Tilly asks.

"Because it does," Camas says.

They walk toward the parking area. Tilly turns back. She scans the playground for a blue crown. Camas reaches out, takes her arm, and leads her away.

CHAPTER 3

Arthur's Hex: The precise geometry of a mechanical tribute

21.4 LBS. – 4.7 GUNS ERASED

Behind Ammo Angels, Trigger Happy Games, and Star-Spangled Everything sits the Liberty Lead Institute. A weathered sign by the gravel entrance reads: *Liberty Lead Institute: Patriotism is a skill set. Classes daily. No refunds. Ask about our wedding discount.*

Inside, Instructor Barry Harlan squints at a clipboard. The range smells of cordite and vending-machine jerky.

"Next shooter up," Barry barks.

Dust steps forward. He wears a baggy camouflage hoodie. Stocky and pale, in his thirties, with choppy bangs, he is quiet in the loud room. He keeps his eyes on the floor. Before stepping to the line, he pulls a folded, dog-eared photograph from his pocket. He stares, then slides it back into the folds of his hoodie.

Barry eyes Dust, then steps back toward another instructor, Levi, and speaks beneath the roar of the ventilation fans. "I teach because I believe in the Second Amendment," he says. "The money helps the retirement fund. But I see someone like that and think, 'That guy should not be holding a gun.'"

Levi watches Dust load a magazine. "We all get guns, though, right?"

"I just hope he's daydreaming of rainbow kittens and aiming downrange," Barry says.

In lane two, a student misses the target entirely and lets out a boisterous whoop. Dust is still. He raises the pistol, eyes steady. He fires.

The shot echoes off the concrete walls. Through the reinforced glass of the observation window, his target slides forward, revealing a single, jagged hole dead center. Lobby chatter stops.

Dust lowers the weapon. His lips move.

High above the valley, on a winding, bermed trail through the pines, Josh and The Bike Guys—Cutter, Joe, and Reeve—take air over wooden stunts, their bicycle tires humming against the dirt.

Crack.

The gunfire from the valley floor reaches them, muffled by the trees. They slow near a cluster of ancient cedars. Just off the trail, three hunters in camo trudge through the brush, rifles slung casually over their shoulders.

"Too close," Reeve mutters. He is in his late 40s with his salt-and-pepper hair. He leans over his handlebars, breathing hard.

"No kidding." Joe's dark wavy hair is damp under his helmet. "Feels jumpy out here lately."

Josh, Camas's husband and Eland's dad, Black in his early 30s with a short-trimmed beard, wipes his brow. "Can we not, just once, have a ride without wondering who's loaded?"

"Or buy flowers at the farmer's market without seeing a pistol hanging on a belt," Cutter adds. Cutter stands 6'2" with a thick red beard. He adjusts the band on his sunglasses.

"You're buying flowers, Cutter?" Reeve teases. "Let me guess. For Miss Larklyn?"

"Maybe." Cutter's face flushes the same shade as his beard. "Dahlias are in season."

The guys laugh.

"We need more people buying flowers," Joe says.

"Damn right," Reeve agrees. He reaches into his pack and pulls out a handful of neon-orange mesh vests. "Which is why I brought these from the shop."

Cutter takes one. "Guess this means I'm officially prey, not predator."

"We're all spooked. Give me the vest. I'd rather be bright than buried." Joe pulls the neon over his jersey.

Arthur Wright, a lean man in his fifties, throws a spry leg over a 1989 Miyata 1400, pushes off, and snaps on a helmet. He leans forward onto the handlebars and pulls away, carving through the Blue Ridge morning like a teen skateboarder.

He pulls onto Grandin Road, Roanoke.

"Damn tourists," he mutters.

He skids to a stop at the first gravel bike he sees. Cables and bar tape are new; the chain is clean. "Probably a full kit wanker."

There is already a spoke card in the rear wheel, advertising a yoga retreat in Floyd County. Arthur pulls the yoga card out. He reads it. He puts it back. Then, he pulls one of his own cards from his chest pocket and slots it into the front wheel.

The card is handmade, milled on a laser cutter he built from parts in 2019.

On one side: A. Wright Precision Machining. On the other side, in smaller type: Bicycle repairs. No miracles. Text for address. 540-yak-bike.

He rolls on, leaving cards throughout town: in the spokes of seven bikes, under two helmets on café tables, under the windshield wiper of a car with a bike rack. Close enough.

He locks his bike to a parking meter and goes inside RND Coffee Lounge. The tables are full and there is a line at the counter.

The bulletin board is a thicket of papers. A lost tortoiseshell cat named Brigadier, sign-up for the Roanoke Valley Half Marathon, a bluegrass jam at the Hotel Roanoke, and piano lessons.

And two, side by side, from the Freedom Front: heavy cardstock, bold font, a screaming eagle holding a rifle and a gavel.

Know your rights. Defend your heritage. Freedom's reunion. Roanoke Pavilion.

Arthur looks at them. He looks around.

He unpins them both, folds them once, and slides them into the recycling bin under the condiment stand. He pins two of his own cards in their place.

Arthur picks up his coffee at the counter. "Thanks, Jill. Don't work too hard this week."

"You got it, Arthur."

He hands her a card. "In case you hear of any emergencies. No prima donnas."

He pulls the last of his cards from his pocket and counts them. Seventeen. He sets them on the vintage turntable near the door.

He puts his coffee cup into an A.Wright-designed steel cage, complete with a latched top for large pothole protection. Riding out of town, a van with a Freedom Front logo cuts him off.

Arthur wobbles, then stabilizes.

He raises his middle finger.

CHAPTER 4

Bike Beats Scroll: Reclaim your world from the digital pull

19.6 LBS. – 4.2 GUNS ERASED

The One More Year offices sit perched over Lake Bijou Nez like a glass-and-timber birdhouse. Below, the Sandglass Rowing Club boathouse hums with the rhythmic clack-slide of early morning practice.

Tilly looks up from her desk at Camas, who taps her keyboard.

"Are you finishing the slides for the Circular Economy conference?" Tilly asks. "They need the deck by five."

"Are you kidding? I can't concentrate on this breakfast muffin, let alone work. Can you?"

"I managed to pull the data for the new campaign," Tilly says. "We have 482 billboards active nationwide, 115 international. Millions of impressions telling people to keep their stuff longer." She exhales.

Camas looks up. Her eyes are rimmed with red. "I'm doom-scrolling. I'm in the dark part of the gun stat world. Do you know how many rounds were fired in Spokane? The caliber?"

Tilly rests a hand on her shoulder.

"I have to know where they come from," Camas whispers, squinting at a grainy photo of a tactical vest. "Who makes them? Who sells the fear? Look at this. 'Protect your castle.' It's a marketing campaign for a war zone."

Tilly pulls out her phone. "I'm calling Moore and Spit."

Across town, Moore and Spit play extreme ping-pong, a game involving the table, the concrete wall, and the side of a dented refrigerator, in a basement of wire nests and bags of stale Flamin' Hot Dill Pickle Cheetos. They move with lanky grace, paddles clicking to the beat from the speakers.

"Nice shot!" Moore yells, diving toward the fridge.

The music is an EDM track by Handbuilt Seconds. Liken Torch's smoky voice raps over a heavy, rhythmic tuba line by her partner Herman 'Bombardon' Ozark.

Moore's phone vibrates on a stack of hard drives. He taps it while the game continues, then freezes at the sound of Tilly's voice. He signals Spit to turn down the volume.

"What is it?" Spit asks.

Moore puts it on speaker. "What's the word?"

"I need your help," Tilly says. "Camas is down in the dumps. She just read a stat that gun violence is the leading cause of death for

American kids, and over nineteen thousand people were lost to gun homicides last year alone."

"It's the Spokane shooting, brother," Moore says to Spit.

Spit rushes to his computer. They sit side-by-side, their multiple monitors in a panoramic digital wall. Moore's chair creaks. His fingers hover over the keys.

"We need to know who's behind the propaganda," Tilly says. "The money, the proliferation. Who's building the mountain of guns?"

"Pro-liff-err…"

"Don't hurt yourself," Moore says. "She means find out who's getting rich off the arms machine. Hack away."

Spit's fingers race. "I'm bouncing off the Spokane local registry… hitting a private server… whoa." He slams the keyboard. YouTube clips flash across the monitors.

"I've got something," Spit says, leaning in. "Chumbeau Culvern. He's the face of a whole org called TRIGGER, the Traditional Rights Institute for Gun Growth, Education, and Recreation."

"Growth?" Tilly repeats.

"It's real," Spit reads. "Tactical summer camps. Teach your kid to stand their ground before they can ride a bike."

Moore grips the back of the chair. "They're all in camo, of course. What are we doing, man?"

"Mappin' the players," Spit says. "This country tears up about a shooting, posts social media for a second, then fizzles like a cow pie on the Outback. That's messed up, man."

"Word," Moore agrees, shaking his head.

"But look at the Queen Bee behind the curtain," Spit says.

A photo fills the screen: a woman in a power suit, holding a gold-plated pistol like a clutch.

"Plinky Borlok," Moore reads. "She wrote *The Armored Household*. She pushes the sovereignty angle and hosts a Freedom's Reunion event in Roanoke next month."

"Looks like she's on the Freedom Front payroll," Spit says. "Every gun event, every rally, she keeps poppin' up. Brass and Brisket Expo. She's their star. I'm looking at her grid right now. Caption says: *Annie Oakley used to shoot cigars right out of her husband's mouth. That's called marital communication, girls. Buy the compact model today.*"

They exchange a glance. Moore leans closer to the phone. "Tilly, the money for this isn't local. It's corporate. It's slick. And they're already planning their next move in Virginia."

"Send the link," Tilly says.

"Time to do more than cry," Moore says.

He raises his hand. Spit meets it. They nod.

The EDM track hits a drop. Camas's voice comes through the phone. "Hey nerds... thanks. Wait, what's that song?"

"Handbuilt Seconds," Moore says. "The track's called 'Forest Drop.' We'll call you when we've got more."

CHAPTER 5

Aquene Glide: Built for iridescent departures

20.6 LBS. – 4.5 GUNS ERASED

Beyond the school garden, in a round building shaped like a snail's shell, sits the Sound Spiral. It is part forest lab, part musical playground.

Stay-cation Music Day: Rabbit Class (two-year-olds) is scrawled on a vintage chalkboard from the original 1894 schoolhouse at Church and Main.

Tiny boots thump. Labeled snack bags swing from fists. Assistant teacher Miss Zina holds her clipboard while twelve toddlers trail behind her. "Climb onto the bus and line up," she says.

The children climb the imaginary steps and march through the picket-fenced yard of the Spiral.

Aquene flops onto her back in a patch of moss. Dampness seeps through her socks. She yells to the sky, "I bringed my bicycle socks!"

"You bringed 'em yesterday too," Eland says solemnly. He kneels beside her and places a yellow leaf on her stomach with the precision of a bird building a nest.

"I did not."

"Did too."

"Not."

"Too."

Pedro watches from a carved cedar bench. He snorts and lifts his head the second he hears the zip of a lunch bag.

Across the grass, a few parents linger.

"Do we think this is safe?" one mom asks, holding her daughter's hand.

"Ow, mommy," her daughter says.

The mother releases her grip.

Miss Zina nods. "It's music day. We took the imaginary bus to our staycation to keep the world close."

The mother kisses her daughter's temple and walks back to the parking lot, her shoulders drooping. Tilly stretches quickly, unties Pedro, and waves to Aquene and Eland. They run off.

Inside the Sound Spiral, everything hums.

The walls are lined with hanging chimes, bowl drums, water flutes, and moss-filled maracas. A fallen larch trunk in the center has been hollowed into a primitive xylophone.

Sunlight filters through stained-glass dragonflies on the ceiling and casts rainbow speckles on the children's cheeks.

Aquene and Eland take stations at the mixing table, a cross-section of an old redwood. They wear headphones of hollowed gourds and woven wool.

"I make the froggie song," Aquene says. She presses a green stone button. A deep ribbiiit echoes through the gourds.

"I make the boat song," Eland says. He turns a wooden crank. It produces the rhythmic creak of oars and the splash of a lake.

They pause, eyes wide. Then, in unison: "Together!!"

They layer bird calls over river stones and hit the larch-log drums with two sticks each. Eland nudges Aquene's socks back toward her with his foot.

"I'mma name our band Pedro the... Pedro!" she declares, flinging a pinecone maraca into the air.

Miss Zina watches it arc into a bowl of cowbells and shaker eggs with a satisfying clunk.

Eland nods sagely. "I play the moon."

Tilly returns and sits under a tree to read a book as she waits for the kids. Pedro naps. A woodpecker joins the percussion from the roof. When one child cries because someone licked their marimba, another offers an apple slice, and the room settles.

Before leaving, the children make music stones, river rocks that hum tones when tapped. Miss Zina tells them to keep them near their beds for nighttime bravery.

Outside, the wind picks up. Leaves skitter across the yard.

Aquene tugs Eland's sleeve. "You hear dat?"

He nods. "It's the forest's music," he whispers.

CHAPTER 6

TRIGGER No More: A machine pointed elsewhere

23.9 LBS. — 5.6 GUNS ERASED

Pinky Borlok sits at the head of a polished walnut table in Freedom Front's temporary command center in rainy Spokane. One heel bounces in vivace tempo. Morning prescription uppers: check.

Chumbeau Culvern, smelling of woody Victory 45-47 cologne, taps a coin against the wood at half tempo, a tiny red eagle flipping to black with every turn of his thumb. On his wrist, a vintage A. Lange & Söhne, wound by hand. His eyes fix on the panoramic display wall.

Plinky slides an ashtray across the table. "Chum, stop that flipping," she says. "It's distracting."

"Plug, what's taking so damn long?" Chumbeau asks.

"The post-Dawn Redwood numbers are right here," the middle-aged analyst says. He touches a tablet, and a heat map of the Pacific Northwest expands in shades of crimson. "Fear-based purchases are up twenty percent in that corridor. The inventory is moving, but we have a sentiment leak."

Chumbeau stops tapping. "Put that on the wall," he barks.

The video appears on the conference room screen. "Who's likely to cause us trouble up there? We've got a lot of skin in those mountains," Chum asks.

Plug pulls out a plaid handkerchief and wipes sweat off his shiny bald head, then swipes the screen. A video window expands, showing two women on bicycles, their baskets overflowing with bright tulips. They are laughing, speaking into a camera. About a hundred riders follow them.

"The Petal Pedal putas," Plinky says, her voice a polished rasp. She leans back, watching the pixelated wheels spin. "They've put a damper on consumerism. They fought plastic, that copper mine in Alaska. Now they've scheduled a community meeting in Sandglass, Idaho."

"I don't think they're promiscuous," Plug says quietly.

Plinky scoffs. "Woke whatevers, then. Trouble in skirts."

"They don't wear skirts, eith—""Plug, drop it!"

"Sandglass is a boutique town," Chumbeau says. "Pottery and gravel bikes."

"It's a trend-setter town," Plinky says. "They don't argue policy. They curate a lifestyle. If they make 'Unweaponed' the new 'Organic,' the brand loses its edge."

A red notification light pulses on Plug's monitor. He leans in. "We just took a ping on the TRIGGER servers. Someone just bypassed the first-tier firewall."

Chumbeau stands. His shadow falls over Plug.

"A breach?" Chumbeau slams the coin onto the table with his

outstretched hand. Plug flinches.

"A clumsy one," Plinky says. "Traceable to a garage in Sandglass. They're digging."

Del, in his fifties, wearing a dark grey Patagonia rain jacket walks in and stands next to the door.

"You're late," Chum barks.

Del stares at the frozen image of Camas and Tilly on the large screen.

"That's my daughter," Del says.

He steps to the polished walnut table and places a manila file down. A wedding photo slides out onto the wood—Camas, radiant, with Josh's arm wrapped tightly around her.

"We never mind when the market plays into cultural anxieties, now do we?" Plinky says, her eyes narrowing at the couple in the photo. "Fear sells across every demographic."

"We're estranged," Del says. "I know Sandglass. My daughter's the heart of it. If she digs, she won't stop until she hits the floorboards."

Plinky turns her chair toward him. "What's the temperature on the ground?"

"They're grieving," Del says. "And when Sandglass grieves, they gather. They're calling it a Circle of Care at the preschool tomorrow night."

Plinky's heel tapping shifts to a hammer beat.

"A Circle of Care," she says. She looks at Chumbeau. "We don't attack the grief. We offer a solution. Draft the letter to the school board and a press release. We donate three Tactical Readiness scholarships. If they want to talk about safety, we'll give them the armor."

She stands.

"And damn it, Del, go home. Watch your daughter."

CHAPTER 7

Saddle of Peace: Broken in for better roads

24.3 LBS. — 5.6 GUNS ERASED

Tilly pedals up the shaded lane. Her breath matches the rhythm of the bear bell swinging on her handlebars and Pedro runs behind. In the trailer, Aquene hums.

Frida kneels in her garden. Bear waves from the porch and sands a piece of driftwood. Frida rises, brushes soil from her knees and walks toward Aquene with open arms.

"My girl," she says. "Did you bring me stories today?"

Aquene unbuckles herself, her blue felt crown slightly lopsided. "P barked at a squirrel, Ama, but it didn't care."

Frida laughs. "That's because squirrels have been here longer than we have. They know when a bark means trouble and when it just means hello."

Bear looks at Tilly as she dismounts. "You've got the storm eyes."

Tilly nods and wipes sweat from her forehead. She embraces Bear, who smells of Clydesdale and Frida's shampoo. Pedro disappears into the trees.

"Come, sit," Frida says.

They sit at a table on the porch.

"I went to Al-Anon," Tilly says.

Frida nods slowly. "And?"

"Alanon says I'm supposed to let go of control. Is that a bad joke? How do you let go of the steering wheel when the road ices over?"

"You're a mother," Frida says. "The first fear came when we carried children on our backs and ran from rifles. Our Lakota brothers and sisters have a word—Wanka Tankan. The Great Mystery. Trusting the mystery is like breathing when the air is thick with smoke. You do it anyway."

Frida motions to a bowl of huckleberries on the table. Tilly takes a few.

"I'm cycling in an endurance race in Virginia," Tilly says.

Frida turns to her.

"I know it won't bring peace," Tilly adds.

"But it may bring clarity. The ancestors ran long distances to warn, to survive, to celebrate. Sometimes movement is our prayer. Just know that no race will outrun grief. But it may carry it better than silence."

Bear bends down to show Aquene a heart-shaped wild ginger flower.

"You're leaving?" Camas slams a binder onto the table. "In the middle of this? We have a community meeting in an hour."

Outside, whitecaps glitter on Lake Bijou Nez.

"It's a race, Cam. It's ten days. I'm not disappearing."

"Ten days is forever right now." Camas crosses her arms. Her neon running tights flash as she paces. "The inbox is full of people asking what we're going to do. They want a response, ideas, something. We figure this stuff out together!"

"You could come. Be my coach, like the old days."

Camas huffs. "I followed you across the country before. I packed my life into a van because you had a vision. Not this time. I've got a kid and a partner. So do you." She looks straight at Tilly. "Also, a social worker is coming to visit for our adoption review. I'm not running away."

"I'm not running away either," Tilly says gently. "I'm riding. You're the CEO, Cam. You'll keep it together."

"I might just fall apart for once and let you watch. Oh wait, you can't watch. You'll be across the country!"

Behind the Herd River Store, Graeme leans over the loading dock and adjusts his touring pack. He looks up as Tilly approaches.

"Where's Aquene?"

"Am I chopped liver?"

Graeme laughs. "That's what happens when you have an adorable kid who looks like her grandpa." Graeme wipes his hands on a greasy rag.

"You ever miss the racing? The 110 percent training?" Tilly asks.

"All the time. But I haven't raced since the accident."

"I'm doing a race. Endurance MTB Nationals in Roanoke. Come with me."

Graeme squints. "You got your Cat 2?"

"I raced three sanctioned events this season. Earned enough points after Whistler."

"Good girl." He turns the crank again.

Tilly watches him work.

"So? You in?"

"You know I'm on the trail every day. But I haven't been racing," Graeme says.

"Masters 55-plus. Any license. You're basically grandfathered in, grandpa."

Graeme laughs. He looks at the river. People exit a raft and wave. He waves back.

"I could go to help you race," he says nonchalantly.

"Sure," Tilly nods. She smiles.

"Roanoke is only a few hours from Fairfax. From the TRIGGER headquarters. Is this a race, or a recon mission? That's where the real guns are."

Tilly looks at the ground. "I'm not going for that."

Graeme sighs and turns his crank. The freewheel buzzes. "Guess I better start climbing stairs on the island again. But I'm not wearing Lycra with flowers. I have a reputation."

The screen door creaks. Liz steps out onto the dock with a stack of flower-patterned bike jerseys. She stops. Her eyes move from the bike to his face.

"What's up? You look like the cat that ate the canary," Liz says.

"Tilly invited me to race with her."

Liz turns to walk back into the store. Graeme looks at Tilly, his face scrunched.

"You could support the ride," Tilly offers.

Liz turns around. She waits.

"Yes, please?" Graeme says quickly, then swings his leg over his bike.

CHAPTER 8

Peace Chain: Driven by life, not lead

24.6 LBS. – 5.8 GUNS ERASED

Folding chairs are set up in arcs in the Meadows School garden amphitheater. Bunting of painted handprints hangs across the porch. At the entrance, a wooden sign reads: *Circle of Care Community Conversation - In the Spirit of Protection and Peace.*

Parents, grandparents, teachers, and townsfolk filter in somberly. A few carry thermoses of herbal tea or water bottles covered with stickers of ski hills and national parks. Mayor Patrick stands at the back of the garden in his jeans and tweed blazer, his arms crossed, listening.

Headmaster Hollis Truemilk stands at the front with a panel: Miss Larklyn, a safety representative, Frida in a handspun vest, and a trauma specialist.

Camas stands at the edge of the crowd. She sees Tilly lock her bike beside Graeme's. Tilly glances her way and waves. Camas does not wave back.

"I don't even know what Tilly's doing here if she's just going to leave us," Camas mutters.

Josh touches her arm. "Let's just listen, Cam."

Hollis steps forward. "Following are the names of those lost at Dawn Redwood Elementary School."

Silence. The distant peck of a woodpecker.

"Olivia Jameson. Mateo Ortega. Mia Tran..."

A reporter stands in front of a mural made of children's handprints in rainbow colors. Bea Leeguard turns off the TV. Her phone rings. She doesn't answer. She picks up her fiddle and stands at the window. Below, the Lincoln Park lagoon is still.

Outside Dawn Redwood Elementary, parents set candles, photographs, and flowers against the front wall. The high school snare drummer stands alone and plays a slow dirge — straight four, a roll on the fourth beat.

A muffled sob escapes from the back. A woman with short dark hair steps forward. "I teach at Dawn Redwood," she says.

The group inhales collectively.

Brock Highside steps toward her. He is a tall man with a weathered face from leading hundreds of people down the whitewater of the Spokane and Moyie rivers. He grabs her hand, and she rests her head against his shoulder for a brief second.

She looks out at the circle. "Words can't express what we're going through," she says, her voice trembling.

Brock wraps an arm around her and holds her steady. He looks at the faces of his neighbors.

"I've seen those kids grow up," he says. "But I am haunted by a kid in my class. After it happened, he looked at me and said, 'There is nothing you can do or say that will convince me that this will not happen again.'"

The names continue to fall.

"…Jamal Greene. Fallon Zaminsky. Henry George… Delia Ramirez. Isaiah King. And Nora Whitefeather."

Camas closes her eyes. Tilly looks toward the animal pens.

"We hold their names," Hollis says. "We hold their memory. Steiner once said, 'Receive the children in reverence, educate them in love, and send them forth in freedom.' From where I sit, that cannot mean arming teachers."

A murmur of agreement ripples through the garden. Some people stiffen.

"I cannot teach with a weapon," Miss Larklyn adds gently. "I will leave this work before I carry one."

A man near the back in a trucker hat clears his throat. "Some of us are just here to keep our ears open," he says.

Several in the group turn to look.

Josh steps forward into the center of the circle. "What if we asked everyone in Sandglass to turn in their guns? Not because someone is coming to take them, but because we chose it. One hundred percent of us."

"Voluntary disarmament?" someone asks. "In this town? We've got more guns than goats."

Liam speaks up. "New Zealand did it. After Christchurch, tens of thousands of weapons were turned in nationwide, in weeks. People chose to."

"They had a government buyback program," someone says. "Money. We've got a whiteboard."

"That's exactly why we should do it here," a teenager in the back row says.

"I was given a four-ten shotgun when I was nine," Camas tells the circle. "I traded it for a snowboard and got grounded for a month. That was the last time I held a gun."

Tilly notices Eland in the back. He rolls back and forth on a balance bike. Her eyes move to a steel frame bike resting against a tree. She whispers in Liam's ear.

Liam steps forward. "What if we turn guns into bikes?"

The room is silent.

"You serious?" Cutter asks.

"We've got enough steel sitting in closets and glove compartments to build a peloton," Liam says.

Joe grins. "Now that's a gear shift."

Soft laughter.

"Brock, you bear hunt. Speak up, man," a man says.

Brock looks across the room. He nods to Tilly.

"Let's write it down," Frida says.

She moves toward the whiteboard. A gray-haired teacher hurries to join her. As the sun dips behind the peaks, the last light catches the fresh ink on the board: *Guns to Bikes*, written in purple paint marker by a shaky hand.

The meeting breaks. Camas catches Tilly at the bike rack. "Are you really riding off while this happens? Your husband just started a revolution."

Tilly exhales and checks the straps on her panniers.

"It was Tilly's idea," Liam says.

"I figured. Now, you're escaping."

"I need to clear my head, Cam. The offer still stands for you to come."

"No way. I've got a town to change." She straightens, shoulders back.

"Understood."

"When you come back, dammit, I expect you to be all in."

"I'm all in now," Tilly says.

Camas raises her eyebrows and walks away toward Josh. "Who starts a revolution and then heads to a race?" she mutters.

Josh catches her hand. "Your best friend does."

Bea puts her fiddle in the case. The snare drum in Spokane is quiet.

CHAPTER 9

The Horizon: Designed for the distance

22.4 LBS. — 5 GUNS ERASED

Graeme moves across the porch of his Opal Island cottage in clipped passes. Bees drift between lilac blossoms. A mud-streaked boot props the red door open under climbing roses.

The mountain bike is clamped in the repair stand, back wheel spinning. A wrench slips. He catches it. Chain grease streaks his knuckles. He wipes them on his shorts and reaches for another tool.

"Breathe," Liz says. She leans against the doorframe, holding two coffee mugs.

Graeme ducks under the vines and grabs a mug. It sloshes.

"You've checked the tire pressure four times," Liz says.

"The Amtrak won't wait." He throws the last item into his pack and zips it.

"Hey," she holds onto his arm to slow him. "You think a race in

Virginia is going to balance the bill for the Spokane shooting?"

Graeme stops. His duffel bag drops to the floor. He looks out at the water of Lake Bijou Nez, reflecting the first light.

"I think if I don't move now, this old dinosaur is going to calcify in bone and soul."

He looks at her.

"What is it?" Liz asks.

He picks up the bag. "I'll tell you at the station. We'll be late. Let's go."

Friends fill the gravel lot at the Sandglass Train Station. Coffee, veggie frittata, and huckleberry muffins waft from the Heaven's Brothers coffee truck. Music plays.

Pedro is buckled into his custom bike trailer behind Liam and Aquene.

Liz's red and ivory 1971 Volkswagen Kombi bus pulls into the lot. Graeme and Liz join the crowd.

Aquene jumps up and down, holding Liam's hand. Tilly rushes from the van and trots to hug and kiss her family. Pedro lets out a dog whimper. Tilly bends to kiss his curly head. "Watch them, P. Don't let anyone cry."

Tilly turns to Liam. "Sweetie, I'll be right back."

Tilly walks toward Camas. She hugs people goodbye. Friends shout, "Good luck!"

Camas's hands are stuffed in her jogger pants' pockets. "You're going to miss the first gun melt. Reeve and I are manning..." she looks down at her cleavage... "and womaning the forge."

The whistle of the Empire Builder echoes across the lake.

Tilly looks to make sure Liam is out of hearing distance. "I'm going to see a place where they make a lot of guns."

Camas lowers her voice. "You're sniffing around the mothership?"

"Don't tell Liam. I will once I'm there."

"Maybe I will, maybe I won't. You'll need me when you find the bastards," Camas says.

"Of course I will."

Tilly hugs Camas. Camas's arms stay at her sides.

The train pulls in. Ike and Cutter hoist the bike boxes up to the porter. Graeme kisses Liz, then steps up into the train.

"What were you going to tell me?" Liz calls over the train's engine .Graeme turns. "I'm..." He pauses. "I'll tell you in Virginia!" He blows her a kiss and enters the train.

Tilly hugs Liz.

Liz whispers, "Find out why this old fart is still running away from me, will you?"

Tilly kisses her cheek.

"I'll be at the station with the van," Liz says, stepping back as the conductor calls for the final boarding.

Tilly steps up into the train. She and Graeme wave to Liz.

Chapter 10

Starforge: Global solidarity on a single frame

22.7 lbs. − 5.2 guns erased

Tilly sits in the back corner of the train observation car, her knees pulled to her chest. Outside, the land is black, deep in the dark stretches of the plains, broken occasionally by the train's headlight sweeping across a fence line or sleeping cattle.

The blue light from her phone illuminates her face. On the screen, the blue door of Dawn Redwood Elementary glows. The handprints look like small, reaching ghosts. Above them are the words: *Every child is a whole world.*

She stares at the red handprint on the far left until the screen dims. She taps it back to life.

The door at the far end of the car hisses open. Graeme enters, bracing himself against the seats as the train lurches over a rough switch.

He stops at the seat across from Tilly.

"Couldn't sleep either?"

"Nope." Graeme slides into the seat. He sets his phone on the table. "My father texted."

Tilly turns her phone over, hiding the mural. The car goes darker. "Out of the blue?"

"My grandmother must have called him. I called her after the shooting."

"I love Vovo."

"So do I. Hard to believe she created Black."

"Is he really that bad?"

Graeme shows her his phone. *Why in hell would a middle-aged man with a bum leg enter a long-distance bicycle race?*

Graeme stares out at the blackness. "When I crashed in Italy, he came to see me in the hospital. He couldn't even look at me. All he cared about was how much the cycling team had cost him."

Light from a passing signal tower flashes across Graeme's face.

"Maybe you can tell Liz some of this," Tilly says.

"She was there."

"I heard you left abruptly. That she found from a teammate."

Graeme looks out the window. He turns back. "What are you looking at?"

Tilly slides her phone back toward the center of the table. She taps the screen. The blue door and the mural reappear.

Graeme looks at the photo. He looks at the yellow handprints, the green ones, the name Leo in small, careful script. He looks at Tilly.

"Twenty-eight lives," Tilly says.

"Puts my accident in perspective."

Tilly nods.

"We're never selling the gun-steel bikes we make," Graeme says.

"Agreed."

At Union Station in Chicago the following morning, the train slows, brakes screaming as it pulls beneath the massive steel and glass canopy. The morning sun is pale through the smog and steam.

Commuters in suits push past, heels clicking on the concrete.

Tilly stands on the platform, her touring bag slung over her shoulder. She looks up at the high, arched ceiling. Beside her, Graeme grips the handles of his gear bags.

"The Cardinal leaves from Gate 14. Hurry. Let's get the bikes," Graeme says, checking the overhead monitor.

Tilly watches a group of schoolchildren in matching yellow shirts lining up near a gate.

She starts to walk around the kids, then slows to walk behind them. Graeme falls in beside her.

CHAPTER 11

The Vovo: A legacy of wisdom on two wheels

26.1 LBS. – 6.3 GUNS ERASED

Vovo, Liam's great-grandmother, sits with a cup of coffee before sunrise in her log home on the Bristol Bay lodge land. Outside, a lone moose trudges past her window. Its breath clouds in the dark.

She eyes her hunting rifle. "Damn it all. Why would I need that old thing anyway?" she says.

Vovo stands, slowly touches her toes, then rises. At 109, her frame is straight, her hands sure. She grabs the rifle, walks to the shed, and opens the gun safe. Inside sit four more hunting rifles, tools that fed three generations of her family.

She loads the guns into a long case and props it against the wall.

"There. Later alligators."

She closes the gun safe, exits the shed, and raises her eyes to the winter moon. "May their deaths not be in vain," she whispers. Then she turns toward the south. A young moose calls for its mother.

"Boys!" Vovo's voice cuts across the baggage claim hall.

Moore nudges Spit. Spit pauses his dance and turns toward the airport crowd.

"Vovo!" the young men say in unison.

Vovo's white hair is in a ponytail. She wears a suede jacket, jeans, worn, shined leather boots, and a silk neck scarf. Her step is lively.

"Help me grab that," she says. She points to a long case circling the carousel.

Moore steps forward.

"I'm holding onto Vov," Spit says, stepping closer.

"You know I hold my own." Vovo says.

Moore lifts the case and grunts. "This is heavy. What's in here?"

"Fishing poles," she says loudly, then whispers, "Rifles."

Spit grabs it from him and immediately drops it to the floor.

Moore laughs. "More CrossFit for you, Mr. Olympia."

Spit hoists it back up. He looks at his bicep.

"How's Alaska?" Moore asks as they walk.

"Waiting on two young bucks to come back for fishing season."

"Are there more girls there now?" Spit asks.

"No."

"Darn," Spit says.

"Why don't you stay in the lower forty-eight with us?" Moore asks.

Vovo smiles. "I'm here to help, aren't I?" She turns to Spit. "Did you bring some 'juana?"

Vovo's phone rings. "Black. I took a black cod out of the freezer for you."

"I'm not calling about dinner. What in the hell did you do with the guns!"

Vovo grabs Spit's headphones and mouths, *hit it.*

She puts her phone near one side of Spit's headphones. "Black, I can't hear you. It's noisy here." She nods to the music. "I'll call you later."

Vovo hands Spit the headphones back.

"Black always scared me," Moore says.

"He scares me a bit too, boys, but he's a good man. Now about that 'juana."

CHAPTER 12

Blue Steel Bolt: A lightning strike of pure utility

20.3 LBS. — 4.4 GUNS ERASED

Tilly and Graeme are three miles into Carvins Cove on a humid climb that opens the race tomorrow.

A sharp crack echoes from Graeme's bike.

Graeme skids to a stop, then looks down at his rear derailleur. The part dangles, bent aluminum and grease.

The hanger has snapped clean.

"Damn. It's toast," Graeme says. "If I can't find a hanger for a vintage Bilenky, I'm done before I pin a number."

Tilly wipes grit from her forehead. "There was a sign a mile back, A. Wright Precision Machining. It looked like a graveyard for tractors."

"No shop stocks an import hanger," Graeme says.

Tilly unzips her jersey pocket and pulls out a card. She turns it over. "It says 'no miracles.' You better hope we don't need one."

"Precision machining isn't bike repair. Nobody here gives a damn about a derailleur."

"You don't know that. You're being a bit dramatic," Tilly says, pushing her bike.

Graeme's cleats stomp the gravel.

CHAPTER 13

The Gear-Grinder: Turning friction into focused momentum

22.6 LBS. — 5.1 GUNS ERASED

A. Wright Precision Machine Shop is a low-slung cement building tucked into the narrow valley. The yard is a museum of rusted parts.

Tilly follows Graeme inside. The junkyard gives way to precision tools, bike parts, and Miles Davis.

Arthur, wearing a grease-stained apron over a button-down shirt with creases down the arms, steps out from behind a computerized mill.

"Bilenky Nor'easter?" Arthur examines Graeme's bike. "Tourlite frame. Phil Wood hubs. You're a long way from Philly, son."

"Hanger snapped. I can't mount the derailleur if the dropout is bent."

Arthur hoists the bike onto a stand. He turns a pedal.

"I can mill a new one. It'll be better than the original. Give me twenty minutes."

He sets up the mill. The room fills with the thin whine of the cutter. Graeme watches every pass.

Tilly moves through the shop of organized tools: tire levers, Allen keys, and torque wrenches knolled like a Marie Kondo sock drawer, a shadow board of vintage bike pumps, and three thermoses in cages bolted to a workbench. Near the CNC mill, specialized end mills and carbide cutters sit in a French-fitted tray, their diameters tiered in a precise geometric array.

Arthur shuts the mill down and blows the chips clear. He holds the new hanger to the light, checks the geometry and sets it against the dropout.

"What brings you out this far for a race?" he asks.

"She dragged me," Graeme answers.

"We dragged each other," Tilly says. "There was a school shooting near home. Twenty-eight kids."

Arthur is quiet. He fits the hanger, then reaches for the derailleur.

Chapter 14

Martha's Revolving: Turning the cycles of history toward home

22.8 LBS. – 5.2 GUNS ERASED

Camas unbuckles Eland from his car seat. The Sandglass Meadows School parking lot hums with the morning chorus: car doors thudding, parents calling out reminders, and the distant chime of the morning bell.

Camas settles Eland into his stroller. He clutches a percussion egg and shakes a rhythm in the air.

"Music time, Mama?" he asks.

"Music time, Eland."

She turns to grab her bag and stops. A fluorescent orange flyer rests under the stroller's handlebar. The paper is cheap; the ink slightly blurred.

"What the eff?"

Your community is being disarmed. Do not let the 'MELT' steal your

47

safety. You cannot protect your family with a bicycle.

The TRIGGER logo sits at the bottom.

Camas pulls the flyer free and looks around. The flyers are taped to the cedar light poles and under the windshield wipers of every Subaru, Honda CRV, and Ford F-150 in the line.

Eland taps the tray with the shaker egg. Thump, thump, thump.

Camas crumples the flyer into a ball and shoves it into her pocket.

CHAPTER 15

The Powder River: Flowing steady through the high country

22.1 LBS. — 5 GUNS ERASED

Graeme is back on the bike and clicks his shoes into the pedals. Arthur wipes the grease from his hands. The new derailleur hanger gleams.

"Check the indexing," Arthur calls out.

Graeme shifts through the gears, his eyes fixed on the cassette. Clack, clack, clack.

He rides a tight circle in the gravel yard, standing up on the pedals to test the torque.

"It's perfect," Graeme says. "Better than the original."

He pulls out his phone. "I didn't bring a wallet. What do I owe you?"

"Don't worry about it," Arthur says. "On the house."

"No, Arthur. We need to pay you," Tilly says.

"You kept me company for an hour. I'll have plenty of business from the race."

"Thanks," Graeme says. He wheels over and shakes Arthur's hand.

Tilly waves and rides down the road.

"You're back in action," Tilly says. "Let's finish the practice ride."

"Did you see the gun tattoo on his thumb?" Graeme asks.

"Huh?"

"I saw it when I shook his hand. It's a black gun with a red universal no symbol over it."

"An anti-gun tat in Roanoke? Why don't we head back tonight? We can bring him something to thank him for the derailleur."

"I can't. I promised Liz we'd have dinner. She wants to talk."

"I'll go then," Tilly says.

"Ask him if he knows anything about the gunmakers."

Tilly rides.

Graeme continues. "And what he thinks of guns into bikes."

Tilly chants softly.

"And if he has insider tips on the race route. And—"

Tilly cuts in. "Are you nervous about the race, or your dinner with Liz?"

"What makes you think I'm nervous?"

CHAPTER 16

The Remembrance One: Original forge machine, built to remember

23.4 LBS. – 5.3 GUNS ERASED

Inside a rusty salvage yard warehouse on the edge of town, heat curls in waves from a reawakened smelter. Sparks pop. Fire crackles. In the Sandglass Reclaim & Forge, dented truck frames and scrap iron rest behind rickety chairs, two vintage couches, and a 1940s Barcalounger.

The Bike Guys and a handful of townspeople chatter. Camas and Reeve stand near the forge and stoke the fire. They wear leather aprons, hoodies, gloves, and goggles. A young man with sun-streaked dreads hands Camas a bellows.

The tall roll-up door rattles open.

Vovo walks in carrying the gun case. Moore and Spit flank her. She wears a kimono jacket over jeans. Her gray hair is loose. She bobs her head to Spit's hip-hop track. The three move forward in silhouette.

Liam carries Aquene over to kiss her. Vovo kisses them both.

Moore and Spit greet the Bike Guys, Reeve, Cutter, and Joe, with handshakes and nods.

"Close the door," Camas says.

Cutter and Joe grab the handles of the sliding door. Brock Highside walks through just before it closes. It groans on its track, clanging shut on the sunset light. Brock shakes Cutter's and Joe's hands.

Ike steps forward. "May I?" He sets Vovo's case on a steel table near the forge.

"Nice jacket," he says to Vovo. He flips the latches. The lid opens.

Vovo steps closer to Reeve. He tips his welding mask up.

Vovo turns to face the room. "If anyone else brought a gun this evening, step forward with its story."

No one moves. The forge breathes.

Camas steps forward. "I'll start. Rites of passage are a good thing, but a gun shouldn't mark them." She sets down a 410 shotgun with an engraved stock. "I shot this twice at a skeet shoot. My dad made me."

Martha, with spun-sugar white hair and a sturdy denim apron, holds a Smith & Wesson revolver with both hands. The gun points downward.

Martha's hands tremble as she places the revolver on the table. "My husband, Flip kept this for forty years. He thought it made us safe. I think it just made him tired. He passed away last year."

Cutter clears his throat. "I enjoyed being with my grandpa, but I didn't like killing birds." He pauses. "When he died, he gave me this."

He places an over/under shotgun beside the others.

Ike speaks next. "I tell Suerte I'm protecting her, but I'm more likely to hurt her with it than without." He adds a pistol to the table.

Moore lifts his hands. "I don't own one."

Spit raises a finger. "I was going to throw in this violent video game, if that won't mess up the alchemy." He riffles through a backpack.

Moore pats him on the back. "You're good, brother."

Pedro barks once.

"I'll track the melt," Cutter offers. He grabs a clipboard. "If we keep track, we'll know if we can scale it."

Reeve nods, then opens the forge. The fire roars. Everyone waits.

He puts the first gun in. Cutter writes on the clipboard.

Gun oil burns off in white smoke. The walnut stock on Vovo's rifle scorches and crackles. The metal darkens.

Reeve and Camas add the other guns one by one.

Vovo watches, her face lit by the glow. The forge roars. The room grows quiet around it.

Vovo sees Brock standing at the side. "Do you have a gun to melt, young man?"

"Not today, ma'am," he answers.Vovo nods.

"Guns to gears," Cutter calls out.

The fire keeps working, popping to the 808 bass.

Ike moves to the side window. He pulls a slat of wood aside and looks out.

"The big white truck," Ike says. "It's back. Just sitting at the corner with the lights killed."

"Let them watch," Camas says. She looks at the glowing, shapeless lump of steel in the fire. "They can't un-melt what's gone."

"Last one for tonight," Reeve calls.

He crosses to Martha. The lug is warm on his upturned palm. The steel shows the marbling of the gunmetal.

He sets it in her hand.

"It'll be the bottom bracket," Reeve says. "The part that takes the most weight."

Martha closes her fingers around it.

Copperhead Commuter: Sinuous grace for the daily migration

23.3 LBS. – 5.4 GUNS ERASED

Tilly pulls up to Arthur's shop in Liz's van. She grabs a paper bag from the front seat, then knocks at the door. No answer.

She tries the door. Locked. She walks around the building and peeks in a window, then tries the front door again.

Leaves rustle and gravel crunches. Tilly jumps.

Arthur pulls up on his bike. "Can I help you?"

"You wouldn't let us pay you. We want to thank you." Tilly holds out the paper bag.

"Biscuits!" Arthur smiles. "You found our specialty."

Arthur unlocks the door, and they go inside. He sets the bag on the workbench and pulls out a biscuit.

"Want one?"

"No, thanks," Tilly says.

He takes a bite. He moves to the mill and starts his work. "Did you really come back just to bring these?"

Tilly leans against the bench. "Graeme saw your tattoo when he shook your hand."

Arthur pulls a measuring tape from his apron pocket and sets a wheel in the truing stand.

"Twenty years at Freedom Front," he says.

"You worked at Freedom Front?"

"I doubt you picked a race in Roanoke just for the climbing."

"We need to know who the players are," Tilly says.

"People have lost more than jobs getting close to these folks. Are you sure?"

"28 kids are dead. I can't stand by."

"We didn't part on the best terms," Arthur says.

"What happened?"

"I overheard a meeting with a couple of their DC lobbyists. When I questioned them about it, they asked me to retire early." The bike wheel spins slowly. "They made me sign a nondisclosure to get a severance."

"Did you sign it?"

A hummingbird flies through the open window and lands on a rainbow-colored set of Allen wrenches. It sits still, then flies out.

"Yeah. But I'm not disclosing now, am I?"

"Of course not."

"Do you remember the French Midland shooting?" Arthur asks.

"That one was bad."

"After that one, there was an uproar. I heard Freedom Front say they were going to bury it in lobbying money." He reaches for a spoke wrench. "Mainly to the suits in DC who treat the Constitution like a parts catalog. Pickin' and choosin' which rights to keep shiny so the kickbacks keep rollin' in. And they weren't just talking about selling more pistols to folks for their nightstands. They were talking about standardization."

"Of what?" Tilly asks.

Arthur sets the wrench down. He looks at Tilly.

"Of fear. One of them said — I'll never forget the sound of his voice — that if they could keep the domestic market hot enough, nobody would ever look at the back of the ledger. A neighborhood in panic is the best screen for a quiet boardroom. It's a closed-loop system. They keep you scared here so you don't look over there."

"Do you have proof?" Tilly asks.

He sets the tape on the bench, opens a drawer, and pulls out a folded floor plan. "Not yet. I grabbed this when I left. I monitor them."

"Can you stop the spinning, please? What's that?"

Arthur stills the wheel. "It's a plan of a storage facility owned by a ghost company that handles Freedom Front's logistics."

He pauses. "I still have a contact there. Woman named Shannon Brestplate. She saw the same stuff I did before they showed me the door."

"Will she talk?"

"I'm not sure. But she's discreet."

Tilly leans over the bench and picks up a grease-covered pen. She writes on a scrap of paper and hands it to Arthur.

"If Shannon's willing, have her call this number. It's my partner, Camas. She can start pulling the thread while I'm on the course."

Arthur takes the paper and puts it in his apron pocket.

He picks up a biscuit and hands it to Tilly.

She takes a bite.

CHAPTER 18

The Melt Zone: From furnace to freedom

23.7 LBS. – 5.8 GUNS ERASED

The gravel of the Matchlove Brewery parking lot crunches under the thin tires of Josh's 1994 Subaru Sambar. Camas kills the engine. Outside, the neon sign of a hop leaf casts green light across their soot-stained faces.

"Everyone's heart still inside their ribs?" Ike asks.

"Check," Moore says from the back of the van.

"Check," Spit adds. "That was messed up. I thought the rig was running us off the road for sure."

They climb out, tense. Camas stretches her neck side to side.

The air is cool and smells of fermenting grain and woodsmoke from the pizza oven. As they walk toward the timber doors, Ike watches the road for the high beams of a white dually.

Inside the brewery, the sound of blades on ice and a muffled stadium roar drifts from the screen above the bar. They find a corner table far from the windows.

"Hi, Andrea, Reeve and the guys are right behind us, plus Liam, Josh and the kids. Oh, and Vovo... we're nine tonight," Camas says. "Who's playing?"

"Ogatok and Salmon Arm," Andrea says, dropping coasters on the table. "The usual, Camas?"

"Two pitchers of IPA for the guys and a N/A ginger beer for me. Three Margherita pizzas. Keep the water coming."

Andrea walks away and does a double take at Camas's dirty hands. Black dust from the forge sits in the creases of her knuckles.

Camas's phone vibrates against the wood of the table. She glances at it and flips it face down. The vibration continues.

"You going to answer that?" Moore asks.

The phone thrums against the table, then stops.

"Nope." Camas looks away.

The door to the brewery swings open. Liam and Josh push the kids in strollers. Vovo pulls off her bicycle helmet and shakes her hair.

Reeve, Cutter, and Joe walk in. The group settles at the table. Reeve pulls his stool closer and leans in.

"We were followed to the Highway 2 turnoff," Reeve says. "He wanted us to know he was there. A real LARPer in a fifty-thousand-dollar truck with a Freedom wrap on the tailgate."

"We were too," Ike says. "A dually. Custom LED bar. It wasn't a local Fudd. Felt like a scout."

"What's a larper?" Vovo asks.

"It's a guy who buys a ten-thousand-dollar mountain bike to ride it to a coffee shop three blocks away," Spit says.

"Larpers are people too," Vovo says.

"Forget this hiding, dammit!" Camas says. She looks around the table. "If we're followed keeping quiet, we might as well step out. We can't change anything lying low."

"How?" Spit asks.

"We name it," she says. "We remind the town. They heard about it at the meeting. But this is different. No more tiptoeing around. From the salvage yard to the cyclocross track to Meadows school—the whole town—this is a melt zone. No weapons. Zero."

"Melt zone. I like it," Reeve says."John Wayne said, 'Courage is being scared to death, but saddling up anyway,'" Spit says. "We're saddled up."

"Since you quoted gun-totin' John Wayne, can I use a gun metaphor when we're getting rid of guns?" Vovo asks.

"Damn right, Vovo," Spit answers.

"Then Spit, darlin,' we're going to give 'em both barrels!"

The Quiet One: Silent steel for the focused path

21.3 LBS. – 4.7 GUNS ERASED

Conversation rises above the hum of the brewpub crowd.

Moore stands. "Be right back." He slides out from the booth.

He walks through the timber doors and into the cool Idaho night.

Moore taps his phone. "You OK? You called Camas."

"Hi bro. I'm OK," Tilly says. "Did she see it?"

Moore stares through the pub glass door. Camas leans over a map with Reeve.

"She's still mad," Tilly says.

"She misses you."

"She's doing a fine job of showing it."

"How can we help?" Moore asks.

"Tell Camas to wait for a call from Arthur."

"Who's that?"

"A bike mechanic who used to work for Freedom Front. He's got a contact."

"What's Camas asking?"

"Camas knows how to get information from people before she knows the question."

Eland and Aquene play in the pub's kids' corner. A low chalkboard wall borders a bin of mismatched toys. Aquene holds a wooden drumstick. She watches the hockey game. A player receives a high-sticking penalty. She bonks Eland on the head.

Eland's face scrunches. His lower lip trembles. He looks Aquene in the eyes, then reaches out, takes the drumstick, and lowers her arm.

He leads her toward a small toy snare drum in the corner and taps the center of the skin. Aquene watches, then mimics the beat, the rhythm finding the bar's bluegrass beat.

At the bar, Syringa wildflowers wrapped in brown paper rest next to Cutter's IPA. Cutter leans against the brass rail,

Miss Larklyn walks in. She takes off her hand-knit poncho.

"Your girlfriend," Joe says, nudging him.

"Not my girlfriend." Cutter smiles. He picks up the flowers, catches her eye, and walks toward her.

In the far corner, Dust sits alone with a full can of beer on the table. His eyes follow Miss Larklyn toward Cutter.

Cutter reaches Miss Larklyn and holds out the flowers.

Dust straightens.

Ogatok scores. A group at the bar cheers.

Dust walks out.

She takes the flowers.

CHAPTER 20

The Bellwether: Proven performance for the leading edge

21.8 LBS. — 4.8 GUNS ERASED

"Bikes on," the lift attendant says.

The morning spring air at the base of The Glarus, known as Ol' Swiss, is sharp and pine-scented. The ski lift hums as the chairs swing around the bullwheel. Camas, Reeve, Ike, and Moore stand in the staging area with mountain bikes, ready for the haul.

Reeve hooks his front tire into the tray of the moving chair. They load in pairs. Camas and Reeve on the lead chair, Ike and Moore behind. As the lift clears the first pylon, the world drops away. Below, the Bear Grass Trail snakes down the mountain through dense Huckleberry bushes.

"We can't walk door-to-door like we're selling cookies," Camas says. Her bike hangs beside her, the frame catching the morning sun. "We need a better way for people to bring their guns."

"The cyclocross race 'Handlecross' is next month," Reeve says, looking out toward the shimmering expanse of Lake Bijou Nez. "It brings in a thousand people. We set up a gun receptacle at the finish line."

On the chair behind them, Ike is leaning back, his eyes scanning the ridgeline. "We need a neutral drop-off. If they bring a piece to the forge, they're putting themselves at risk. But if we have a bin at the trailhead? At the Matchlove? It's community service."

They reach the summit, the chairs swinging wide at the top station. They offload, tires hitting the wooden ramp and rolling toward the Ol' Swiss Cafe. The deck is massive, overlooking the lake and Sandglass valley.

"About time," Spit says, putting his hair up into a ponytail.

"I need my beauty sleep," Camas says. "What have you figured out?"

Vovo turns to Spit. He nods for her to go ahead. Cutter and Joe roll up breathless and take the stairs two at a time. They slide in.

"There can be no shaming. If this is going to work, somehow there needs to always be complete acceptance of all types," Vovo says.

"You came up with that?" Moore looks at Spit.

"Remember when you said I needed to ski and snowboard?" Spit asks.

"Yep."

"Until I knew you respected boarders, I was opposed, man."

"I remember," Moore says.

"Then, when I saw you had some pow skills on a board, I decided I could give it a try."

"Wasn't it for the girls?"

"That too."

"We're not going to start shooting things to make them feel better though, are we?" Joe asks.

"No, good question. But we need to make a pact that we won't disparage gun owners in our Melt Zone campaign," Vovo says.

"Not even privately?" Ike asks.

"Well, we're not angels, are we? Everyone agreed?" Vovo holds her hand to the circle of the group. The others stretch to place their hands on top.

"Spit?" Vovo prompts.

"Gun owners are people too on three," Spit calls. "One, two… three."

Their voices join. "Gun owners are people too!" The sound carries down the mountain.

People turn to look. A man puts his hand to his hip with a squint.

On the far side of the Ol' Swiss deck, below the tree line where the groomed trail gives way to scrub, Dust stomps awkwardly in heavy exercise rucksack riding high. He grunts each step, does a single burpee, then looks around at the bustling café. No one is watching him.

He sits, takes out his phone. His cheeks puff with each tap. *Kkhh. Kkhh.*

"Let's get to work." Camas spreads a town map on a weathered picnic table. She puts her multi-tool and water bottle on either corner.

"Look at the layout," she says, pointing. "From the Meadows School to the forge. We mark the perimeter with the stickers. Every person who turns in a piece gets a Melt Zone badge. We make it a point of pride. A status symbol."

"Like a reverse gun permit," Moore says, nodding.

"I was thinking of some retro-style buttons, like the old vote for blank buttons, but a mock Melt Zone reverse gun permit is perfect," Camas says.

"Why not both?" Ike asks.

Camas nods "On the way up, Reeve had the idea of using the Handlecross riders to crowd-source the steel. We make the Melt Zone part of the community fun, as big as the dog sled keg pull and the Thanksgiving fishing derby."

"June 6th is ten days out. That's tight," Joe says.

Reeve stands up, checking the air pressure in his tires with a rhythmic hiss-hiss. "The first frame is almost ready for the jig. If we can get ten more pieces of high-quality Chromoly by Friday, we can have the first Melt Zone prototype rolling by the race."

"We need a low-profile way for people to contribute. For people who don't want to be seen dropping their block or broomstick," Ike says.

"I can do it," Vovo says. "I'll de-cool myself, grab a couple other fabulous elder queens, and we'll cruise on our tricycles with kayak trailers."

"That should work," Reeve says. "Thanks, Vovo."

"Liam, Josh and the kids are at the huckleberry park at Glarus

Village. I texted Josh to go see the GM about putting a gun drop box on the hill."

"Bold," Cutter says.

"It's hard to say no to cute toddlers."

Camas looks toward the Selkirks. "Let's ride."

The group gathers its packs and heads toward the trailhead.

"Vov and I are going to ride the lift down," Spit says.

"I ride the flats," Vovo smiles.

Moore kisses her on the cheek.

"Stumpy's and Jumpy's," Cutter yells.

"And Squirrel Master," Ike calls.

The gang drops in, one by one. The lift hum fades. Freehubs whir.

The mountain goes quiet as the next empty chair sweeps up behind them. Spit and Vovo step into the line, the metal bar coming down with a steady click. Their feet dangle over the treetops, swinging together into the wide, blue descent.

The Spark Gap: Bridging the distance with electric intent

20.8 LBS. – 4.5 GUNS ERASED

Tilly pulls on her trail shoes in the motel parking lot. The sun heats the pavement. She throws a small pack over her shoulder and walks toward downtown.

Grandin Road is waking up. Coffee shops, a bookstore, a yoga studio with a sandwich board out front. She scrolls her phone as she walks. Camas has sent three voice memos. She ignores them.

A gun shop sits between a barbershop and a florist. The shop's window display is orderly. A handwritten card reads: Your right to carry in public spaces is under attack. We stand with you. Beside it, a stack of printed flyers: Rally to Restore Second Amendment Access, Mill Mountain Park, Saturday 10am.

Tilly stops. Reads it again.

Second Amendment.

She keeps walking.

A coffee shop has a small speaker above the door. Gillian Welch's voice sings a Bob Dylan song. *Bullet holes and scars between the spaces...* Tilly slows, then moves on.

She stops on the sidewalk. A woman steps around her.

She puts her phone in her pocket and finds the Star Trail.

The switchbacks above the city are steep, and she pushes into them hard, arms pumping.

At the overlook she stops, hands on her knees. Roanoke spreads out in the valley below, blue-gray in the morning haze. A hawk rides a thermal.

Tilly's phone rings.

"I talked to Breastplate."

Tilly waits.

"Are you there?" Camas asks.

"No hello?"

A pause. "Hello. Are you OK?"

The wind picks up at the overlook. Tilly catches her breath. The hawk tilts and slides sideways across the air.

"I'm trail running."

"It's a rest day," Camas says.

"I'm surprised you know that."

"Always your coach. I can hear your VO2 max dropping through the roaming charges. Why are you running?"

"I walked through Roanoke this morning," Tilly says. "There's a lawsuit here. Pro-gun groups are suing the city to carry guns in the parks. There's a rally at Mill Mountain on Saturday. A man carried a pistol past a woman with a stroller and she thanked him for holding the door."

Tilly exhales. "And I saw a bumper sticker: *An armed society is a polite society*. Eight days since Dawn Redwood. Nothing. No flowers. No photographs. Nothing for those kids."

"You need P."

Tilly laughs.

"I'm serious. They should have a rent-a-dog. You're on a trip, you're bored, depressed, need trail protection. Bingo. Rent-a-Ruff. You pick the breed, the energy level, the size. You get a dog that matches your crisis."

"Cam."

"There's a market. We're leaving money on the table. I'd franchise it."

"Cam."

"Small, medium, large, or the Pedro Special. It's an emotional support water dog that judges your pace and licks your shins."

"Camas." Tilly smiles. "Stay focused."

"I am focused. We're not twiddling our thumbs over here."

"Are we making bikes yet?"

"We?" Camas says. "You're riding bikes. I'm making them. But yes. Almost there."

Tilly takes a drink from her water bottle. "OK."

"OK," Camas says. "And we just locked in a gravel race for a collection campaign. Reeve's got the jig ready. Arthur's contact gave me enough to pull the thread. Things are moving."

The hawk is gone.

"I think I might have something from the racecourse tomorrow," Tilly says. "Something we can use."

"Good. Now listen to me. You do a few downward dogs at the top of that hill, you run down that trail and pretend Pedro's at your heels, and you get us some stellar recon on those gun bastards."

"Copy that, sista."

Tilly pockets the phone, stretches her arms wide, and looks up at the sky. She turns toward the trail and runs.

CHAPTER 22

The Crucible: Pure intent in every revolution

25.3 LBS. — 6.1 GUNS ERASED

The Sandglass Reclaim and Forge is quiet. The street is dark beyond the roll-up door. A map of the Handlecross course is drawn on a vintage schoolhouse chalkboard in the corner.

A Glock 17 slide hits the steel workbench with a sharp, hollow *clack*. Reeve leaves it where it lands. He studies it like it's a puzzle piece from the wrong box. Moonlight shines through the high window.

"It's tool steel," Reeve says. "Hardened. High carbon." He gestures to the induction furnace, where a rifle barrel glows cherry red. "If I TIG weld this to a standard down tube, the heat-affected zone is going to turn into glass. Tilly hits a rock at forty miles an hour and the frame snaps."

Ike looks from the bucket of stripped receivers to the digital scale. "So we're sitting on forty pounds of useless junk?"

"We can't weld it," Camas says. She's perched on a stool, her thumb tracing the edge of a 3D-printed plastic sleeve. "We lug it."

Reeve looks up, squinting through the soot. "Lugs? Like a vintage Colnago?"

"Exactly." Camas tosses him the sleeve. "We don't melt the gun steel into the frame. We cast the gun steel *into* these lugs. We use the firearms as the joints—the elbows and the knees of the bike. Low-heat brass brazing keeps the metallurgy intact."

Reeve turns the plastic sleeve in his gloved hand. He looks at the pile of weapons, then back to the jig. "A weapon-grade skeleton," he mutters. He picks up the tongs, his eyes on a Winchester barrel. "Alright. Let's pour some joints."

Camas picks up a colored chalkboard marker, circles the Handle-cross finish line, and writes 'gun drop: bike feedstock.'

Josh walks in holding Eland.

"You two are still up?" Camas asks.

"We came to bring you home," Josh says. He kisses Camas.

Eland wriggles out of Josh's arms. He pulls the marker from his mother's hand and draws a tiny heart on her leg, the purple ink bleeding into the black lines of the mountain range tattooed on her thigh.

CHAPTER 23

The Blueprint: Forged according to plan

21.9 LBS. – 4.8 GUNS ERASED

Found pinned above the jig at the forge.

RECLAIM-1 FRAME SPECIFICATION

Project Code: MZ-01

Primary Material: Mixed Ballistic Alloys: 4130, 8620, and Tool Steels

Tube Set: Repurposed rifle barrels, wall thickness verified by micrometer

Goal: A rideable, race-worthy frame. No cracks. No excuses.

I. FEEDSTOCK PREPARATION

Strip all polymers, optics, and lubricants from the donor firearms. Separate high-carbon slides from chromoly-molybdenum barrels. They behave differently in the furnace and the frame needs to know the difference.

One lug = one-third of a Remington 700. Weigh accordingly.

II. THE CASTING SOLUTION

Gun steel is too hard to weld into a standard frame without creating brittle fracture points in the heat-affected zone. The solution is to stop welding and start casting.

Print custom lug geometry (head tube, bottom bracket, seat cluster) in high-resolution burn-out resin. Coat in refractory ceramic slurry and cure. Fire the shells in a kiln to melt the resin out completely, leaving a precise voided mold.

Melt the feedstock in the induction furnace at 1550°C. Gravity-pour into the hot ceramic shell.

Crack the ceramic once cooled.

What's inside is a seamless, weapon-grade steel socket. The elbows and knees of the bike.

III. THE COLD-HEART JOINT

Sleeve the tubes into the cast lugs. Leave a 1/16-inch gap for capillary action. Apply flux.

Heat the joint to a dull cherry, 650°C. Feed 56% silver solder into the gap and watch it wick. The silver finds every void on its own. Do not rush it. Do not exceed the melting point of the base steel.

When it cools, clear-coat the frame.

Do not paint it. The marbling in the steel is the ballistic history of the material. Every alloy that went into the furnace left a mark. That's the point. Let it show.

NOTE FOR THE SMITH

In a Hollywood movie this process takes six minutes and looks like a music video.

In the Sandglass Forge, with three sleep-deprived engineers, a borrowed kiln, and a dangerous amount of caffeine, it takes forty-eight hours of straight labor.

Do not rush the melt.

The bike has to hold a person going downhill at speed.

Get it right.

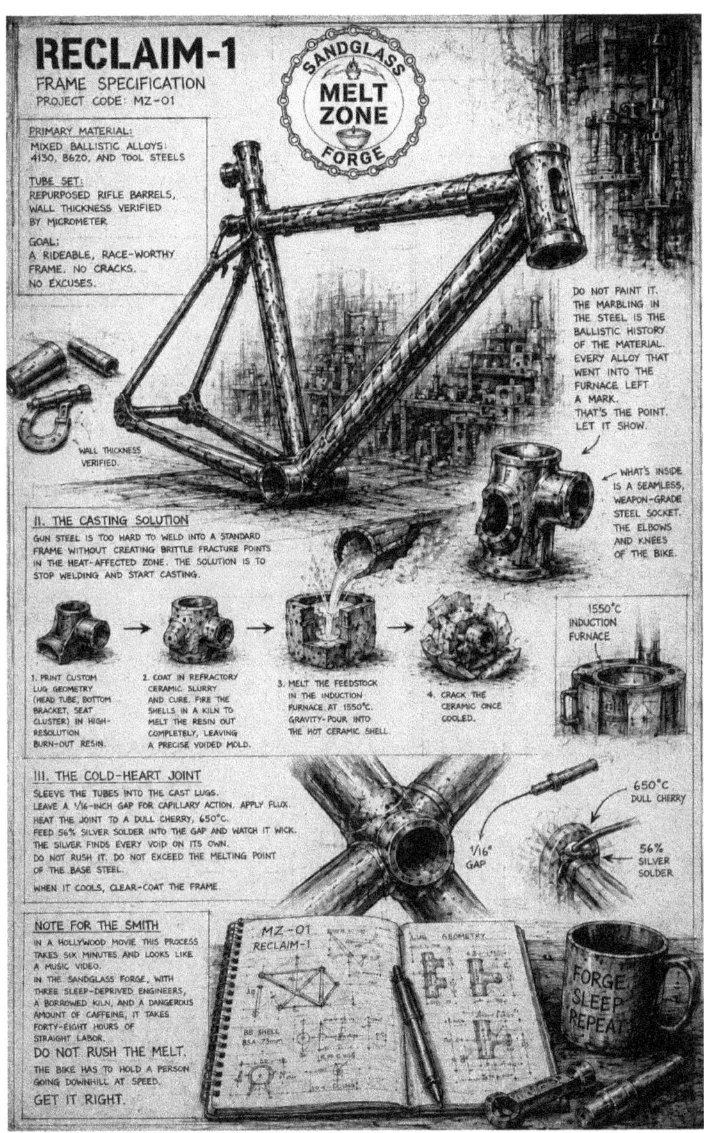
RECLAIM-1
FRAME SPECIFICATION
PROJECT CODE: MZ-01

SANDGLASS
MELT ZONE
FORGE

PRIMARY MATERIAL:
MIXED BALLISTIC ALLOYS:
4130, 8620, AND TOOL STEELS

TUBE SET:
REPURPOSED RIFLE BARRELS,
WALL THICKNESS VERIFIED
BY MICROMETER

GOAL:
A RIDEABLE, RACE-WORTHY
FRAME. NO CRACKS.
NO EXCUSES.

DO NOT PAINT IT.
THE MARBLING IN
THE STEEL IS THE
BALLISTIC HISTORY
OF THE MATERIAL.
EVERY ALLOY THAT
WENT INTO THE
FURNACE LEFT
A MARK.
THAT'S THE POINT.
LET IT SHOW.

WALL THICKNESS
VERIFIED.

WHAT'S INSIDE
IS A SEAMLESS,
WEAPON-GRADE
STEEL SOCKET.
THE ELBOWS
AND KNEES
OF THE BIKE.

II. THE CASTING SOLUTION
GUN STEEL IS TOO HARD TO WELD INTO A STANDARD
FRAME WITHOUT CREATING BRITTLE FRACTURE POINTS
IN THE HEAT-AFFECTED ZONE. THE SOLUTION IS TO
STOP WELDING AND START CASTING.

1. PRINT CUSTOM
LUG GEOMETRY
(HEAD TUBE, BOTTOM
BRACKET, SEAT
CLUSTER) IN HIGH-
RESOLUTION
BURN-OUT RESIN.

2. COAT IN REFRACTORY
CERAMIC SLURRY
AND CURE. FIRE THE
SHELLS IN A KILN TO
MELT THE RESIN OUT
COMPLETELY, LEAVING
A PRECISE VOIDED MOLD.

3. MELT THE FEEDSTOCK
IN THE INDUCTION
FURNACE AT 1550°C.
GRAVITY-POUR INTO
THE HOT CERAMIC SHELL.

4. CRACK THE
CERAMIC ONCE
COOLED.

1550°C
INDUCTION
FURNACE

III. THE COLD-HEART JOINT
SLEEVE THE TUBES INTO THE CAST LUGS.
LEAVE A 1/16-INCH GAP FOR CAPILLARY ACTION. APPLY FLUX.
HEAT THE JOINT TO A DULL CHERRY, 650°C.
FEED 56% SILVER SOLDER INTO THE GAP AND WATCH IT WICK.
THE SILVER FINDS EVERY VOID ON ITS OWN.
DO NOT RUSH IT. DO NOT EXCEED THE MELTING POINT
OF THE BASE STEEL.

WHEN IT COOLS, CLEAR-COAT THE FRAME.

1/16"
GAP

650°C
DULL CHERRY

56%
SILVER
SOLDER

NOTE FOR THE SMITH
IN A HOLLYWOOD MOVIE THIS PROCESS
TAKES SIX MINUTES AND LOOKS LIKE
A MUSIC VIDEO.
IN THE SANDGLASS FORGE, WITH
THREE SLEEP-DEPRIVED ENGINEERS,
A BORROWED KILN, AND A DANGEROUS
AMOUNT OF CAFFEINE, IT TAKES
FORTY-EIGHT HOURS OF
STRAIGHT LABOR.
DO NOT RUSH THE MELT.
THE BIKE HAS TO HOLD A PERSON
GOING DOWNHILL AT SPEED.
GET IT RIGHT.

MZ-01
RECLAIM-1

LUG GEOMETRY

BB SHELL
BSA 73mm

FORGE
SLEEP
REPEAT

CHAPTER 24

The Iron Syringa: Resilience forged into every petal

24.1 LBS. – 5.7 GUNS ERASED

The humidity in the Blue Ridge foothills is a physical weight. A thousand riders stand in a mass of carbon fiber and Lycra, their tires crunching on the gravel at the neutral start on Day One of the race.

Graeme sits on his bike three rows back from the front. His hands rest lightly on the hoods, his eyes fixed on the rear tire of the rider in front of him.

Tilly is ten yards to his left, her mountain bike a rugged anomaly in a field of gravel racers. She adjusts her helmet strap, then her glove. *Velcro rip. Reset. Velcro rip.* She catches Graeme's eye for a split second. He gives a single, sharp nod.

The official raises the starter's pistol.

Crack.

The canopy thins, opening into a blinding stretch of a fire road on the Blue Ridge Trail. The dirt is baked hard, a white ribbon vibrating under their tires. Tilly and Graeme ride shoulder-to-shoulder, the only sound the rhythmic *whir-click-whir* of the drivetrains.

"Saved oxygen won't help you if your head drifts off the line," Graeme says. His face is streaked with sweat and grit.

Tilly shifts her weight, her tires finding a smoother line in the dust. "How was the dinner? I see you survived it."

"Liz wants me to move off the island," Graeme says. He stares straight ahead, eyes hidden behind dark lenses. "She wants a five-year plan."

"Liam and I have been telling you to move closer for years. And your granddaughter too."

"She told me she isn't a pit crew. She's a partner."

"It's kind of cool that she's both," Tilly says.

"It's an ultimatum. A yes or no before we leave Virginia." Graeme stands on the pedals for a brief climb.

"You know, Frida once told me that an ultimatum is just a fence built by someone who's afraid you're going to run."

"I'm not going to run," Graeme says.

"Maybe you should make sure she knows that."

They crest the hilltop, and the flat fire road suddenly gives way to a jagged, descending spine. The view opens. The Shenandoah Valley spreads below them, the spring oaks so dense they look like moss from this height. The trail narrows into The Gauntlet, a technical descent where the Appalachian roots and rocks rattle the frames.

Tilly drops her seat post. Wind whistles through the vents of her helmet. They plunge into a stand of skeletal ghost trees, pines stripped by a long-ago fire, standing silver and leafless against the forest floor.

"Let's change the subject," Graeme calls out over the chatter of the rocks. "What'd you find out at Arthur's?"

A root catches Tilly's front wheel. She corrects and catches up.

"He has a contact at Freedom Front," she shouts.

The trail pitches steeper.

"If Liz finds out we're scouting a shadow corp instead of listing my cottage on Airbnb, we might lose our support crew of one."

Camas's Hammer: Rugged durability for the wild terrain

27.2 LBS. – 6.8 GUNS ERASED

Camas texts Tilly. 11:42 AM

You're probably screaming down a trail right now, but read this when you hit the flats.

Shannon came through.

The drop point is a storage facility off Route 11, south of the race finish. Unit 1938. Look for the Mac the Yak mural on the side of the building.

I'm uploading her digital key-fob clone to your phone now. It'll bypass the gate and the unit lock, but only for a twenty-minute window.

Be careful, Til. Get the footage and get out!

Tilly texts Camas. 11:48 AM

Key fob received. Why is she helping us?

Camas to Tilly. 11:51 AM

She has a son. He's starting at the high school in the fall. She spent a decade shipping components that turned the world into a minefield.

Tilly pulls her bike into the shade of a massive, ancient oak just past the twelve-mile marker. Her chest heaves, lungs burning. She taps her phone.

"Arthur. I have the address. Route 11. Mac the Yak mural."

"I know the place. I'll meet you at the back perimeter. Don't use the main entrance. There's a gap in the chain-link by the drainage ditch. I'll have bolt cutters if the fob glitches. What's your start time tomorrow?"

"Seven. I can break off at the twelve-mile marker. Thirty minutes from the gate."

"Mac the Yak at seven-forty. Don't be late."

CHAPTER 26

The King Sting: Small-frame chopper with big energy

9.2 LBS. — 1.8 GUNS ERASED

Camas sits at the scarred wooden desk in the middle of the forge, a cup of lukewarm tea beside her. Cooling steel from the morning's pour ticks as it contracts.

Her phone buzzes. Then again. A string of notifications from the Sandglass Community Forum and the Herd River local group.

She taps a link.

A professionally edited video launches. The title cards flicker in high-contrast black and red: *Know the agitators.*

The video cuts to a grainy, long-lens shot of Tilly and Camas at Heaven's Brothers café. They are leaning over a map. Plinky Borlok's voiceover, infomercial-smooth.

"Is your community being used? Outside activists are moving into Sandglass, exploiting local tragedies to push a radical disarmament agenda. They don't want to save your children. They want to take your heritage."

The video ends with a shot of the Melt Zone sticker being scraped off a pole by a gloved hand.

Camas watches it twice.

Camas taps her phone. *Dad.*

"Camas?" Del's voice is tired and gravelly.

"What the hell, Dad? You're in with the second protectorate shit?"

Silence.

"We haven't talked since Mom died," Camas says. "I don't know why you're calling me now."

"You called me."

"You know what I mean," Camas says.

"I want to know what you and your Injun friend and your brown hubby are doing going up against guns. Are you nuts? You're painting a target on your chest."

"It's not about the guns, Dad. It's about the people who own you. Is that why you're calling? To give me a corporate script?"

"You're playing with fire in a town full of dry wood. Those videos are a light breeze. The storm is coming."

The line goes dead.

Camas stares at the screen. She sets the phone face-down on the anvil.

The roll-up door rattles. Moore ducks under it first, a paper bag from Heaven's Brothers held above his head. Spit follows, beatboxing into the cinderblock echo. Cutter comes in sideways with a wheel, Joe behind him. Ike comes in last, kitty backpack zipped to the chin, Suerte's black face pressed against the mesh.

"Lunch burritos," Moore announces. He sets the bag on the workbench.

"Liam texted that he and Josh are at the Sound Spiral with the kids. He'll catch the team update later," Reeve says.

Cutter leans the wheel against the wall. "You OK, Camas?"

Camas turns her phone over and taps the video.

They watch in silence. Plinky's voiceover fills the forge. The video ends.

"My dad's in it," Camas says.

"Bummer. I'm sorry," Moore says.

"Handlecross sign-ups are bad," Spit says. "Forty-two. We targeted three hundred."

"The video isn't helping," Joe says.

"They're saying online the bikes aren't real," Moore adds. "That we're burning guns for content and there's nothing to show."

Camas looks at the jig.

Ike unzips his pack. Suerte jumps to the floor. Ike reaches back in. He pulls out the pirate flag from his houseboat, salt-stiffened and sun-bleached, the skull grinning crookedly above cross bones. He raises it above his head with both hands.

The group looks at him.

"Yes, Calico Ike," Camas says. "Did you want to speak?"

"I'll ride a gun bike at the race."

Joe coughs. "I mean. Yeah."

"You're the PR queen, Cam," Moore says. "If we announce we're riding gun-steel bikes in the Handlecross, can you make some noise?"

"That should help attendance," Spit says.

Excited chatter. Cutter nods. Joe pulls out his phone.

"Hold on." Reeve's voice cuts through from the back. "We haven't made a bike yet. Not one. How many are we talking?"

Ike raises the Jolly Roger.

The group laughs.

"You should ride, Camas," Cutter says.

"Damn right." She looks at Reeve. "You in?"

"No, thanks. I'll man the gun drop with Bear."

"A teacher would help the cause," Joe offers. "Maybe that tall guy at the community meeting. Tilly's friend."

"Brock," Camas says. "He's more of a water man than a mountain biker. We can ask him."

Moore looks around. "OK. Ike, Camas, teacher guy. That's three."

"It'll be tight," Reeve says. "We'll target four as padding." Suerte reappears from under the workbench.

Ike scoops her up and raises the pirate flag toward Reeve. "Weld her on, matey."

The Resonator: Feel the vibration of harmony

21.7 LBS. – 4.9 GUNS ERASED

Moore and Spit sit sprawled on a sofa patched with industrial duct tape and scraps of indigo denim. A video call is open on Spit's phone. The screen shows a grainy view of a chaotic workshop in Portland.

On the screen, Liken Torch leans into the camera, her hair a wild halo of black curls. Behind her, Bombardon is visible, hoisting a vintage tuba onto a workbench.

"We saw the footage of the Melt on the forge channels," Liken says. "We've been waiting for someone to actually light the furnace. That gun-bike video you dropped on socials is exploding. We're in."

"Whoop!" Spit kicks his legs out. "Handbuilt Seconds are coming to Sandglass!"

Moore leans toward the screen. "We'll be ready for you. We've got the feedstock prepped, and the designs locked. You'll beat-box-wrangle the Melt Zone stragglers."

"Seven days. We're bringing the acoustics," Liken says. "Tell Sandglass to get the steel hot."

The screen goes black. Moore looks at Spit.

"A week. If we don't have the bikes finished by the time they pull into the driveway, we're just a couple of guys with a loud hobby."

Moore grabs his phone. "Camas, the band confirmed."

"Good work," she says.

Moore taps the track *Speak to my Gun.* "Let's hope people show up."

CHAPTER 28

The Frida: Art and grit in every defiant stroke

20.2 LBS. – 4.4 GUNS ERASED

The Herd River Store is a maze of organic grain bins and locally cured meats, Snake River wines and Selle Valley honey. Vovo is behind the counter, her hands moving through a stack of invoices, when the bell over the door jingles.

Barry Harlan stands at the counter with a gallon of milk. Away from the shooting range, his shoulders sag. He holds his phone up, the screen frozen on a frame of Plinky Borlok's video.

"You see this, Vovo?" Barry asks. "Tilly and Camas from the forge. This video says they're plants. Coming in to tell us how to live. Making us look like monsters while they play with our heritage."

Vovo doesn't look at the phone. She looks Barry dead in the eye, her glasses sliding slightly down her nose.

"I see a man holding a phone when he should be paying for his milk," Vovo says.

Barry's eyes narrow. "The town's talking, Vovo. People don't like being played for fools by outsiders with a political axe to grind. You're letting them use your store as a clubhouse."

"They're not outsiders. You know that." Vovo rests her weathered hands on the wood of the counter. "You want to talk about heritage? Count the guns your grandfather had at the Wood V ranch, then count how many your nephews Scooter and Ryder have. Then come back and tell me who's being played."

Barry thumps the milk onto the counter and fumbles with his wallet. He drops a twenty and doesn't wait for his change.

"Times are changing," he says, grabbing the jug. "Even for you."

"The seasons change every year," Vovo says as the door swings shut. "Doesn't mean the mountain moves."

The Texas Tavern is a brightly lit slot of a diner, ten stools jammed against a porcelain counter that smells of griddled onions and bleach.

Graeme shifts his weight on the end stool and lets out a groan. He massages his right thigh. A full bowl of chili sits in front of him.

"Going to make it?" Tilly asks.

"The race start is at seven AM. The humidity is currently eighty-four percent. I am merely calculating the electrolyte degradation."

"You look like you're waiting for a dental appointment," she says.

The screen door jingles.

A small entourage steps into the narrow aisle behind them, two men in matching black tactical polos, radio mic loops on the shoulders, the slight bulk of a holster at the waist, and Plinky Borlok, talking over her shoulder to one of the men. She wears a tailored linen blazer, her blonde hair perfectly smooth despite the midnight air.

"The Roanoke park permit's already locked," Plinky says, her voice carrying that same infomercial-smooth cadence from the video. "We just need the digital assets from the morning rally to go live before the afternoon press meetup."

"Order up!" the cook shouts.

Plinky leans over the counter between Graeme and a local, flashing a polished smile at the short-order cook. "Two Cheesy Westerns to go. Extra relish."

Graeme shifts slightly away from her linen sleeve.

"We have a problem though. Breastplate's a canary," Plinky tells the men.

Tilly keeps her head down, her thumb tapping her phone screen beneath the counter line. Plinky's expensive perfume cuts through the grease of the griddle.

The cook slides the brown paper bags across the counter. Plinky drops a crisp bill, nods to her team, and the screen door jingles shut behind them.

"Who was that?" Graeme asks, finally taking a small bite of chili.

"Freedom in bra holster."

Tilly to Arthur. 8:17 PM

Borlok's here at the Texas Tavern. Heard her say Breastplate's a canary. Still on for tomorrow?

Arthur to Tilly. 8:19 PM

If they change the fob code, we'll know at the gate. Stay the course is my vote.

Tilly to Arthur 8:20 PM

Roger.

Miss Larklyn sits at her small writing desk, the window overlooking the Meadow School playground.

She opens the Sandglass Community Page on her tablet. The feed is full of Tilly the Traitor reposts and orange TRIGGER icons.

She types:

I have taught the children of this valley for forty years. I know the hearts that build and the hearts that break. Tilly and Camas are builders. The Melt is not about taking; it is about making something new from what has hurt us. I stand with the forge.

She hits post.

Two miles away, in the dim light of a parked sedan at the edge of the forest, a screen glows.

Dust sits in the driver's seat, his eyes bloodshot. He scrolls through the new posts on the community page. He stops at Miss Larklyn's name. He stares at the text, his thumb hovering over the glass.

He puts the car in gear and pulls onto the gravel road.

CHAPTER 29

Skyframe: Lightweight precision for the soaring spirit

18.4 LBS. – 3.9 GUNS ERASED

D ay Two of the Endurance Mountain Bike race support lane is a corridor of dust and shouting. To the right, the lead riders have scattered into the scrub, dust rising where each one drops over the ridge. Tilly keeps her mountain bike steady on the shoulder, her eyes fixed on the turnoff for the next checkpoint, just ahead to the right.

She makes a quick left instead.

She pedals hard, navigating the suburban sprawl toward the storage address.

"I'm a lost tourist," she says under her breath. "I took a wrong turn at the Walmart. I don't know anything about logistics. I'm sorry. I don't know an Arthur Wright."

She passes the massive big box store, just beyond the garden center, tucked behind dying poplars. The walls are beige corrugated metal, the perimeter strung with rusted concertina wire.

Tilly rolls her bike toward the keypad.

She punches the numbers: 061063. She waits. A green light blinks once.

The gate slides open.

Arthur stands by the back door of the van labeled Happy Haven Pool & Spa. He wears a neon-yellow safety vest, a floppy khaki sun hat that hides his face, and thick wraparound mirrored sunglasses. He holds a clipboard and a pool skimmer.

"You're late for the cleaning, Sheila," Arthur says.

"I got tied up on the golf course."

Arthur gestures with the clipboard toward the far end of the building, where a fading Mac the Yak grins from the cinderblock, an oar in his mouth, horn through a baseball, Blue Ridge pine trees running along his hairline. Unit 1938 is next to him.

"The security cameras here have a blind spot every ninety seconds when the swivel resets," Arthur says. "We have forty seconds left on this loop. Move."

They reach the unit. Tilly pulls out her phone and holds it to the reader. It blinks green.

The metal door grinds as it rolls into the ceiling.

Arthur moves quickly through the musty air straight toward two massive, olive-drab tanker desks.

"Thought there'd be servers," Tilly says, her flashlight on a stack of file cabinets.

"The server is the screen door. It's what you show the burglars so they think they've found the house," Arthur says. He pats the top of the nearest desk. "But this is the foundation. Steelcase 1954. You can't hack a Steelcase. You can't delete what's inside with a magnet. This is where the old men kept the things they were too stubborn to burn."

He yanks the bottom drawer. It screams, metal-on-metal.

He pulls out a thick, accordion-style folder bound in rotting elastic. The label is hand-typed: Operation BB Gun (1969-1974).

Tilly leans in. Her light hits a memo on Freedom Front letterhead. The paper is so thin it is translucent.

She photographs it. She keeps going.

Midway through the folder, a map. Hand-drawn, dated 1972. The Pacific Northwest. Red circles around two towns.

She photographs it. Moves on.

At the back of the folder, a single bright white page is held by a rusted paperclip. Laser-printed, current.

Three columns: Region. Designation. Status.

She scans down. Coeur d'Alene. Kalispell. Missoula. Spokane.

She stops.

Sandglass-Herd River Corridor. Phase 1 Enforcement Zone. Status: Active.

She looks back at the 1972 map. At the two red circles.

She raises her phone.

Click. Click. Click.

Arthur sips from his thermos. "You ever think about biscuits?"

"I'm photographing."

"A real biscuit, a southern biscuit, it's built on a paradox. Light enough to float, heavy enough to hold the gravy. Too airy, the gravy turns it to mush. Too hard, it's a hockey puck." He sweeps his flashlight across the cabinets. "The Big Six: LockStep, RayThorn, Freedom Front, BowSing, Universal Statics, Northgrip. They're the gravy. They needed something heavy and permanent to hold their weight. They needed us to be the biscuit."

Tilly doesn't look up. She photographs another page.

"Fifty years," she says. "Same map."

"They just changed the paper it was printed on."

She looks at the folder. Hundreds of pages. She has photographed maybe twelve.

Arthur's hand closes on her arm. "Now."

"I need two more minutes."

"We don't have two more minutes."

She takes one more photograph.

"Freight truck's one minute out." Arthur pulls her toward the door.

CHAPTER 30

Cinder Cycle: Rising from the ash of the old world

23.8 LBS. – 5.6 GUNS ERASED

The preschoolers are inside Meadows School for quiet time, the low hum of a cello through the classroom speakers. Frida sits in the grass, her Thursday circle, children stringing beads around her.

Cream-colored Barnaby the alpaca grazes in the pasture, a fixture of the school's biodynamics lessons.

In the tree line above the pasture, Dust stands still. He looks at the school, then the alpaca. He shoves the photograph back into his pocket.

He raises the rifle.

Crack.

Dust walks into the woods.

The school doors fly open. Headmaster Hollis stands there, his face ashen. "Down! Everybody down!"

Frida is still. She whispers, "Hold tight to your beads," as she scans. Miss Larklyn bumps the headmaster's shoulder rushing past. She falls to her knees, pulling as many children as she can under her arms.

Frida looks toward the shot. She sees Barnaby stumble. The alpaca lets out a high, whistling bray and collapses onto his side into huckleberry brush.

She walks into the woods, listening.

Frida presses her hand into Barnaby's shoulder. Bright blood wells up between her fingers.

She chants.

Thirty minutes later, Sheriff Miller's cruiser idles at the edge of the schoolyard, its blue and red lights strobing against the cedar siding. The children are huddled in the library, the quiet time now silence.

Miller walks the fence line. He stops near a cluster of pine trees fifty yards from the pasture. He kneels, his knees cracking.

He picks up a brass casing in the dirt with a gloved hand and turns it over in the sun. A .308. A hunting round. High-velocity.

Barnaby is loaded into the vet's trailer. Frida washes the blood off her hands in the outdoor garden sink.

Miller looks at the ridgeline and trees of the Glarus.

He slips the casing into a plastic evidence bag.

CHAPTER 31

The Unloader: Weaponless soul ride

26.8 LBS. – 6.5 GUNS ERASED

Liz keeps her hands at ten and two, her gaze fixed on the white lines of the Interstate headed east. The dashboard glow paints her face in soft amber. Graeme is slumped in the passenger seat of the Kombi, his eyes closed. The van is a steady, vibrating capsule of yellow light cutting through the Virginia dark.

"They shot Barnaby," Liz says.

Graeme's eyes open. He straightens. "What? Barnaby? At the school? What about the kids?"

"No other injuries, thank God. Frida called while you were at the finish line," Liz says. "He's with the vet now. The kids are shaken but safe."

"Liam called me at the finish line," Tilly says from the back seat. "Who did it?"

Liz glances in the rearview. "Someone saw Dust in the tree line.

That's all Miller has."

Graeme looks out the side window at the blurred silhouettes of the trees. He clears his throat. "Liz. About that talk. The one we were supposed to have on the way back. Can I get an extension?"

Liz reaches over, her hand resting on his forearm. "Of course."

Liz presses a button and Madeleine Peyroux fills the van.

The air in the private dining room of The Lodge at Prim Farm smells of beeswax and aged leather. Outside the arched windows, guest tree houses are sprinkled over an expanse of lawn. The Virginia ridges turn purple in the fading light.

Plinky stands by the fireplace, snapping the breech of a custom over-under shotgun open and shut. Open. Shut. Open. Shut.

"No, I don't know who the hell did it."

"Our gun." Chumbeau sits at the heavy mahogany table, a cleaning mat rolled out before him. A disassembled vintage double-barrel sits in pieces—barrels, forend, receiver—beside a small, high-resolution portable monitor."

"The shooter is a loose wire. He's not ours," Plinky says.

"Says here he shot a fluffy therapy animal at a preschool."

"Alpaca," Plug says from the corner of the room.

"I don't care about the taxonomy. It's on the news," Plinky says.

Chumbeau uses a fine brass pick to clear a speck of carbon from the shotgun's firing pin channel. His movements are slow, deliberate, completely detached from the broadcast metrics.

"Only local affiliates, Calm down. Pull the school safety training radio spots we planned for 72 hours. Let the sentiment settle. No big deal."

Plinky steps toward the table. "We can't drop the momentum now. The forge is leveraging the outrage."

Chumbeau taps the monitor screen with the tip of the brass pick. A surveillance photograph fills the display, a shot through the open bay doors of the Sandglass Forge, long lens, high contrast. It zeroes in on the frame jig. A set of gun barrels is visible, sliced and cleanly wrapped into a bicycle's head tube cluster.

"Look at that weld," Chum says.

Plinky leans over the table, her shadow falling across the steel components of his shotgun.

"It's a silly bicycle frame."

"Look at the lug work. Hand-filed chromoly brazed directly to heavy ordnance steel. You know the heat differential required to marry those two tensile strengths without warping the throat? Whoever is running that torch is a master craftsman. Nobody in our production facilities files by hand anymore. It's a lost art."

"You're the lug, Chum." Plinky steps back. "Can't you see they're melting our inventory?"

Chumbeau sets the brass pick down with a soft click. "You work for me. I've been watching this town before you had your first pimple. Let it go."

Chumbeau picks up the receiver of the broken-down shotgun, checking the tolerances of the hinge pin with his thumb. He zooms in closer on the hand-filed lug of the gun bike, his thumb tracing the shape of the steel on the glass.

Plinky turns to leave. She grabs Plug's elbow. "Come on, I've got something for you to do," she says under her breath.

Plug follows her. The heavy door clicks shut behind them.

Camas posts a video of the flashing amber lights of the vet's truck pulling away from the preschool. She taps and scrolls.

Her phone buzzes in her palm. A text from Del.

Heard about the llama shooting. You and the boy OK?

Camas stares at the screen.

We're safe.

Three dots appear. Then they stop.

She puts the phone face-down.

CHAPTER 32

Spokane Spirit: Runs rapids on two wheels

24.5 LBS. — 5.7 GUNS ERASED

"Vovo? What are you doing here? You can't be on the line without ears," Barry Harlan says.

He fumbles a pair of plastic muffs off a hook and hands them to her. Vovo takes them, holds them like a basket of eggs, and puts them on.

Barry gestures for her to follow him. They walk behind a row of shooters into Barry's office. He closes the door.

Vovo sits down in front of Harlan's desk. Barry waits.

She picks up a wrinkled brochure from the desk and reads gun specs.

"Oh, nuts. You're here about that alpaca."

Vovo looks him in the eye.

"You can't pin that on me. The range won't take the rap for your anti-gun crazies."

Vovo is quiet.

"You're taking my students, Vovo. Twelve this month alone." He moves behind his desk, then stops. He sits in the chair next to her.

"I watched Dust for months," Barry says. "I saw that look. Target fixation. We see it sometimes." Barry looks at the vintage pinup calendar on the wall. "I didn't say anything. I told myself he was just quiet and that it wasn't my business as long as he paid his fees and hit the paper. But I saw it. I've seen it before."

"Ever thought you might want to teach fishing?" Vovo puts her hand on Barry's arm. "I don't know much about karma, but don't you have guns in this place that don't work anymore?"

"Maybe."

"Bring them to the Melt Zone. Nobody has to know they came from Liberty Lead."

Barry stands. "Got to get back. Put the headphones on."

Brass casings hit the floor as Vovo strides past Barry. She turns, taps a lumberjack-sized man on the shoulder. She takes his bolt-action rifle, raises it to her shoulder, and shoots.

Bullseye.

CHAPTER 33

Forge Together: Built by your neighbors, for your world

25.7 LBS. – 6.2 GUNS ERASED

Before first light, Ike walks alone to the lockbox at the Herd River trailhead. The box is bolted to a cedar post between the bike map and the bear canister instructions. He unlocks it.

Inside, wrapped in a dish towel printed with sunflowers, is a pistol. No note.

The river below is loud with snowmelt. Ike tucks the wrapped bundle into his pack and walks back toward the forge.

At the Sound Spiral, Miss Zina has pushed the larch-log xylophone to one side to make room. Parents and teachers file in after drop-off, guns in cases and cloth bags, setting them on the redwood cross-section where the children mix sounds on music days. Miss Zina documents each one on her clipboard.

Headmaster Hollis stands in the doorway, his hands in his pockets.

"Where's your drop, Hollis?" a parent asks.

"My wife won't let me," Hollis says.

He steps aside to let the next person through.

Reeve guides Roy's grip to the torch. Roy is a rancher in his sixties, hands like worked leather.

"You're not melting anything yet," Reeve says. "Just getting warm."

The flame is small and blue at the center. Roy holds it steady.

"When it goes orange," Reeve says, "that's when it starts to change."

Roy watches the steel.

Spit films a matte-black AR-15 receiver at 120 frames per second under a ring light. The gun lowers into the crucible. In slow motion, it unravels, becoming a glowing pool of orange. He cuts to the Melt Zone leaderboard, the number climbing, then to the Bike Guys racing down a trail.

#GunsForGears Spit types and hits post.

Eight women at the Cedar Street Yoga Studio sit in a circle on their mats, a collection of small handguns arranged in the center — a pearl-handled .22, a rose-gold compact, a matte lilac pistol with a custom grip.

Frida sits at the top of the circle, her eyes closed.

Bear fills the doorway. He carries a wooden box, unfinished, still smelling of sawdust. One by one, the women silently place their guns inside.

"Is this legal?" a woman in dusty rose tights says to the woman beside her, setting her pistol in the box.

Bear looks at Frida. She opens her eyes and meets his.

He takes the box.

Frida lights a bundle of sage and walks the circle. Then she follows Bear to the door, the smoke trailing behind him.

The Glarus Lodge sits at the edge of the tree line, its log walls chinked with white mortar, a row of trophy elk mounts visible through the dining room window. The staff are a particular Sandglass blend of bearded line cooks, high-bun servers, a busser with a nose ring and a Melt Zone badge on his apron.

In the employee corridor near the walk-in cooler, a drop box is bolted to the wall between the coat hooks and the staff schedule.

A well-heeled elk hunter in a pressed Filson vest comes through the wrong door. He stops and reads the sign above the box.

The busser looks up from his phone. "Melt Zone gun drop. The forge makes bikes out of them."

The hunter looks at the box. He goes to his truck and comes back with a rifle. The lodge manager unlocks the box and puts the gun inside, then latches and locks it.

The hunter takes a photo and texts his wife.

The hardware store on Main opens at seven. By eight a Melt Zone badge sits in the corner of the front window. By noon there are three more. The barbershop, the feed store, dental office above the bike path.

Del stands on the far side of Main, watching a man carry a rifle case through the forge door at the end of the road. He passes Heaven's Brothers café where the Melt Zone drop box sits outside near the outdoor rock-climbing wall. He puts his hand on his gun belt and lifts the pistol over the box. A few locals stare.

He shoves the gun back into the holster, grabs a Dawn Redwood memorial poster off the community bulletin board, crumples it, and shoves it into the drop box. He walks away fast.

A child's face on the corner of the poster sticks out of the box.

Mayor Patrick slows outside the forge on his lunch break. A bicycle frame hangs on its hook inside the open bay door, rotating in the heat draft.

Late that night, the mobile forge sits in the shadows behind the Matchlove Brewery. A truck pulls up, lights off. A man drops a heavy duffel bag into the bin and takes a sticker from the dispenser. He watches for a moment as Joe, silhouetted by the trailer's pilot light, begins the work.

The spark hits the dark air.

Another gun gone.

Peace Pledge: A promise kept with every mile

21.5 LBS. — 4.8 GUNS ERASED

The Kombi pulls into Tilly's drive and the front door of the house flies open. Pedro, Liam, and Aquene race out of the house and reach the van door just as Tilly slides it open.

Tilly pulls them all in, breathing in the scent of fried potatoes, soap, and dog treats. She kisses the top of Aquene's head, then her cheek, then Pedro's curls, then Liam's lips.

"I missed you," Liam says.

"I missed you more."

Tilly rides through the forge doors, Aquene in the trailer behind her. Camas looks up from a workbench covered with bicycle components, a row of standard parts, each paired with rougher Melt Zone versions.

Ike scoops up Aquene and hugs Tilly.

"How is Eland?" Tilly asks. "Was he close?"

Camas walks toward her, wiping her soot-stained hands on a rag. "He's okay. He was at the drawing station in the back with his music headphones on."

Tilly steps off her bike. She hugs Camas firmly."Moore and Spit went through everything you sent," Camas says. "You got more than you thought."

Moore has a laptop open on the workbench. He turns it toward Tilly. On the screen, the memo fills the frame.

Spit straightens, pulls one side of his headphones off his ear and down to his neck. He reads aloud.

"First one's handwritten. Paper-clipped to the front."

R,

BB Gun is a go. BB guns first, then the .22, then the whole catalog. That's the ladder. We keep the bottom rung cheap and we own the top.

LockStep, RayThorn, BowSing, Universal Statics, and Northgrip are following our lead. First mover advantage. Here's the memo for the board. Keep it clean. They don't need to know how the sausage gets made.

C. Culvern, Southwest Regional, 1969

"Eff me," Camas says.

"There's more?" Reeve asks.

"Yup. Memo's on Freedom Front letterhead." Spit nods to the beat.

"Move over." Moore bumps Spit aside and takes the laptop.

Moore reads aloud.

TO: Board of Directors, Project TRIGGER Liaison

RE: Tactical Saturation as Public Relations

The anti-war sentiment regarding Southeast Asia presents a long-term risk to our export margins. To mitigate this, we propose a Civilian Vanguard initiative. By licensing surplus frame designs to domestic subsidiaries like TRIGGER, we normalize the aesthetic of the battlefield in the American home.

"Maybe we needed Spit's beat version. This is dark," Reeve says.

Moore continues.

If the citizen views our technology as an essential tool for his own home, he will cease to view it as a moral violation when used on foreign shores. A nation of owners cannot be a nation of objectors.

The room is quiet.

Moore swipes to the next image. A map of the valley, dated 1972. Red circles around Sandglass and Herd River.

He swipes again. The Phase 1 table. Current. Laser-printed. Sandglass-Herd River Corridor. Status: Active.

"Sandglass has been their gun experiment since before Ike was born," Moore says.

Camas stares at the guns waiting for the crucible.

"That's fucked up."

CHAPTER 35

Sherwood Forest: Untamable spirit for the deep woods

25.4 LBS. – 6 GUNS ERASED

Hollis Truemilk greets parents at the firehouse community hall. Tilly and Camas ride up with their kids.

"Thanks for changing locations," Tilly says.

"Miss Frantel will be teaching today."

"Where's Miss Larklyn?" Camas asks.

"She's sick. First time in eleven years."

Cutter sits next to Miss Larklyn in her living room. She pulls out a photograph of herself at the school, printed on regular paper. She sets it on the table in front of Cutter.

"This was under my windshield wiper."

Cutter looks at it. He turns it face-down.

"Do you have someone who can stay with you tonight?" he asks.

"My sister's in Coeur d'Alene. She's headed over."

"I'll be on the porch."

At midnight, Reeve takes Cutter's place on the porch. Joe sits in his truck a block down.

Camas's phone rings. She picks up.

"This is Chumbeau Culvern. I know your father."

"Who are you?"

"I think a better question is, 'Why are *you* getting mixed up in guns?'"

"I'm not mixed up in guns. I'm mixed up in bicycles."

"Don't you have an adoption review meeting coming up? Maybe they won't like your son's proximity to firearms."

Camas is silent. She waves Josh toward the back door. He takes Eland out.

"I think we've gotten off on the wrong foot. I'd like to have a conversation about what's best for Sandglass," Chumbeau says.

"Listen to me, you son of a bitch. Mumbo Chumbo, whoever you are. I'm doing this for my son. You can take your guns and melt them or shove them where the barrel doesn't shine."

Camas hangs up.

Dust sits in the sedan on a dirt road outside of town. The passenger seat holds a gas station coffee cup, a crumpled Liberty Lead schedule, and a game case with a man in dark sunglasses and assault rifles in both hands.

CHAPTER 36

The Zero Frame: The absolute absence of conflict

19.8 LBS. – 4.4 GUNS ERASED

Ms. Bea Leeguard

National Association of Classroom Teachers

355 Fourth Avenue SW

Chicago, IL 60007

Dear Ms. Leeguard,

I am a teacher at Dawn Redwood Elementary. For twelve years, I've taught long division and Inland Northwest history. I never expected to be a human shield.

Within the last month, I have been asked to do two things that seemed impossible: carry a loaded weapon in my classroom, and imagine a world without one.

I have hunted the Selkirks with my parents and grandparents since I was a child.

I have spent the last few weeks in a forge here in Sandglass. I have watched locals hand over their firearms and watched those weapons lose their shape in the furnace and become bicycles.

I have seen the end of 28 lives in the hallways where I work.

Tomorrow night, I am adding my rifle to the Melt Zone. It is the gun my father gave me. I would rather be a teacher who builds something than a teacher who waits to shoot.

The National Association of Classroom Teachers represents four million teachers. We are told the solution to school violence is to turn us into an armed militia. What if four million teachers helped their communities turn guns into something useful? Maybe then we wouldn't need to turn our schools into fortresses.

I am asking the Association to start a Melt Zone at every school.

Sincerely,
Brock Highside
Teacher, Dawn Redwood Elementary

Turning Point: Engineering the moment the world shifted

20.9 LBS. — 4.6 GUNS ERASED

Melt Zone badges sit in neat stacks on the long table inside the forge. Two safety pins are fastened to the corners of recycled denim with white screen printed letters on a black circle,

"Hey, turn up the tunes. That's Liken's new song, 'No gun for me. No gun for you." Spit puts safety pins on the badges.

"These new badges rock," Spit says.

Moore nods. "Feels like a real thing now."

Camas slides into the seat across from them.

"It is a real thing," she says. "We start at nine. Table opens at eight. No chaos. No speeches. Just the gravel race and the gun drop."

"For each gun dropped, we document carefully, then secure it." Reeve says.

"Then repeat." Camas taps the stack. "Everyone gets a badge. Not just people dropping guns. If they believe in the mission, you pin it on."

"Make sure you tell them it's their ticket to the melt music after the race," Cutter adds.

Josh stands at the counter with Eland leaning against his leg, half-asleep. Aquene drums on the table with two straws, a steady cadence.

The forge door rolls open. "Sorry we're late," Tilly says. Graeme and Liz follow behind her.

"Where are the bikes?" Graeme asks.

"Can't you give a proper greeting?" Liz scolds.

"I'm excited," Graeme says.

"Me too," Tilly says.

"Me three!" Aquene shouts.

"What bikes?" Camas teases.

Camas nods at Reeve.

Reeve and Cutter disappear into the back.

Reeve rolls the first bike out. Ike's bike is a low-slung, pirate-inspired build with the Jolly Roger mounted on a mast pole at the rear, sun-bleached, the skull grinning at eye level.

The melt team erupts into cheers and whistles.

Ike grabs the top bar. "Pirates plunder the rich under the cover of their own courage."

Cutter rolls the next bike over to Camas. Hers has a neon-yellow frame and strips of hot pink ribbon looped through the handlebars.

A fresh round of clapping breaks out.

From the back of the seat post, a cluster of small metal circles jangles on a length of chain, reflecting the forge fire.

Tilly stares. She steps closer. "Are those what I think they are?"

"Yep," Camas says. "My leftover boob necklaces from Burning Man."

A wave of warm laughter goes around the forge.

Reeve rolls a third bike out from the back, a tall Hetchins-inspired steel build. Welded on the head tube is a small steel apple, smoothed and shaped by hand.

"Brock's," Reeve says.

"Nice work," Tilly says.

Moore looks around. "I thought you were making four."

From outside, faint at first, jumping brass notes in a swing beat, Cab Calloway's Jumpin' Jive roll across the forge yard.

The side door bangs open.

Vovo rolls in on a steel bike with a vintage radio mounted to the frame pumping. A small electric battery is fastened to the down tube, powering the motor and the radio. She does a slow loop around the interior of the forge, one hand on the bars and the other snapping to the beat.

She stops in the center of the room.

"While you're out getting dusty," she says, "I'll ride around the grounds showing off The Vovo."

The room goes wild with whistles and stomping. Spit pulls his headphones down to clap above his head and Eland abandons his straws and claps with both hands. Reeve lets out a sharp finger whistle.

Ike, Camas, and Vovo take the bikes out through the roll-up door into the evening air. Cutter rides Brock's. The forge team spills out after them onto the gravel, drinks in hand.

Miss Larklyn rounds the corner on a Gazelle Tour Populair bike. She rolls to a stop at the edge of the group. She lowers the kickstand with her heel.

She reaches into the front basket and hands Camas a bright orange flyer.

Camas takes it. Vovo turns her music off.

Freedom's Reunion. Sandglass Pavilion. June 6th. One Day Only. Because Heritage Doesn't Melt.

"They picked our date," Reeve says.

"Of course they did." Camas looks at the paper, then at Miss Larklyn, then at the team. She tucks the flyer into her pocket.

"Bastards."

CHAPTER 38

The Requiem Rider: Carry the names that move us forward

23.1 LBS. – 5.3 GUNS ERASED

The cyclocross course runs through the lower meadow and back up through the pines, finishing on the gravel flat. By nine in the morning, the course tape is up, the hay bales are stacked at the barriers, and chain lube, coffee, and banjo music fill the air.

A banner-sized Melt Zone sign hangs above the gun receiving station twenty feet from the finish line. The forge-built steel table holds a locked receiving box, clipboards, and a camera on a tripod.

Liz, Frida, Reeve, Bear, and Mayor Patrick greet cyclists and townspeople holding guns of all shapes and sizes. A sandwich board reads:

Step 1: Declare your firearm to the volunteer at the table.

Step 2: The volunteer renders the firearm safe and documents make, model, and serial number.

Step 3: You receive your Melt Zone certificate and badge.

Step 4: The firearm is locked in the receiving box pending transfer to the forge.

The line is orderly with old friends catching up and new friends being made. Some hold cases, some bags. One man unbuckles his pistol holster and sets it on the table without ceremony. Bear documents each one. Liz checks the lock on the receiving box after every third deposit.

At the edge of the flat, three women in matching puffer vests set up a ring light on a tripod next to a man with a press badge from the Spokane Recorder. A fourth person, young, in a Melt Zone badge and expensive trail runners, holds a phone on a stabilizer and pans slowly across the receiving line.

Near the start line, Vovo sits on her Melt Zone bike in the morning sun. A small crowd gathers around her: children, two older couples, and a teenage girl in camo. Vovo talks with her hands.

Ike rolls to the start line first. The out-of-town riders do a double take at the skull and crossbones flag.

"Hey, is that one of those gun bikes?"

"It's a bike. No more guns," Ike says.

"I don't have any guns, man, but I support the cause."

Ike leans toward him and pins a Melt Zone badge to his jersey.

A young girl watching the start pulls her friend's sleeve. She points. The influencer films.

Camas rolls up beside Ike on her gun bike. She unzips her jersey to show her Melt Zone badge pinned to her kit underneath.

The Spokane Recorder photographer raises his camera.

"Are those gun-steel frames?" the man with the press badge asks Camas.

"Every gram," Camas says.

A ripple moves through the crowd near the course entrance. People step aside.

Brock Highside walks his bike cautiously toward the starting line. He wears a kayaking helmet, round and red, with a Dawn Redwood sticker on the back, a bright green vest buckled firmly over his race number.

Camas looks at him. "Brock."

"Yeah."

"Is that a life vest?"

"Thought the padding might help."

"You'll fit in fine," Ike says.

The starting horn sounds.

The first wave goes out in a roar of tires on gravel, the course swallowing them into the meadow. Ike's Jolly Roger disappears into the dust. Camas is right behind him, the necklaces jangling until the course bends and the sound fades. Brock goes out steady, then wobbles, head down.

Ike takes the back loop at the hay bales and coasts straight to the receiving table. He drops his bike against the fence and ties on a forge apron.

Graeme rolls to the line in the second wave. His Bilenky is caked to the downtube with Virginia red clay that hasn't fully washed out. He unclips a shoe at the course tape, nodding at Tilly beside him.

"Hey, old man, you rocked the Virginia race," Tilly says.

Graeme smiles. "Not too bad."

Riders pass through the finish line, mud splattered. Tilly finishes. Camas and Graeme are right behind her. Liz hands Graeme a water bottle. He drinks half and pours the rest over his head.

Josh, Eland, Liam, and Aquene cheer.

Barry Harlan stands at the edge of the flat. He watches the gun bikes cooling against the fence. He watches Brock pin a Melt Zone badge next to his race number.

The Sheriff's vehicle pulls onto the gravel flat. Two deputies follow in a second car. Sheriff Miller walks toward the receiving station, his hat in his hand.

"Patrick," he says.

Miller hands him the paperwork.

The mayor reads it twice.

Emergency Temporary Restraining Order.

Petitioner: Freedom Front Legal Defense Fund.

Grounds: unlicensed firearms transfer and destruction in violation of the Gun Control Act, Section 922.

Effective immediately pending hearing. All firearms transfer activity to cease.

The mayor looks at the receiving line. Twenty people still waiting, their cases and bags in their hands.

"Sheriff." The mayor shakes his head.

"I'm sorry, Mayor. I have to serve it."

The mayor walks to the receiving table and leans in to Ike.

Ike straightens and looks at the line. "Folks." His voice carries across the flat. "We have to pause the receiving. There's a legal order."

People look at each other. A woman near the front sets her paper bag carefully on the ground, then picks it back up. A man in a hunting vest nods slowly. A teenager looks at his father.

"We'll be back," Ike says. "Thank you for being here. Every one of you."

Bear moves toward the sheriff.

"Bear, leave it," Ike says.

Bear stops. He looks at Miller. Miller looks at the ground.

Spit and Moore come running across the flat toward Tilly and Camas.

"They shut us down."

CHAPTER 39

BB Fun: Kinetic joy in every rolling loop

13.7 LBS. – 2.7 GUNS ERASED

"What the fuck?" Camas says.

Across the gravel, people are walking back to their cars, guns in hand and Melt Zone badges on their chests.

"Easy sista," Tilly says.

Tilly turns to the crowd. "Wait!" She steps up onto a hay bale.

Camas steps up onto the bale.

Vovo stands over her bike and reaches down to turn the music off. She nods to Tilly.

"Don't leave yet. You drove out here this morning and whether or not you left a gun, you wanted to," Tilly calls.

"Damn right!" Camas says. "We want to give you something."

Tilly jumps down. She runs to the badge tray. She looks at Aquene and Eland. "Come here, you two."

Tilly fills their hands with badges.

The kids walk down the line, handing out one badge at a time. Frida follows the toddlers through the crowd.

Bear lumbers up.

"Looked like you were going to dig a hole and put Miller in it," Camas says.

"I'm a peaceful man." Bear smiles. "Tell all those people to bring their guns to the forge tonight."

"But it's illegal," Tilly says.

"Don't doubt Coyote."

"Huh?" Camas says.

"I'll explain later," Tilly says. She hugs Bear.

Camas grabs her hand as she steps back, and they race to Aquene and Eland, scooping them up with kisses.

CHAPTER 40

The Steel Sycamore: Natural architecture grown for the trail

24.9 LBS. – 5.8 GUNS ERASED

Outside the forge, the line stretches past the bay door and into the gravel lot. Most have badges pinned to their jackets. Some are still pinning them on as they walk up. Many hold gun cases. Some just the badge.

Sheriff Miller's cruiser is parked at the edge of the lot, engine off. He stands beside it, watching the line grow.

The forge fire is banked low for the evening.

Ike's gun bike leans against the forge wall near the bay door, the Jolly Roger catching the light. A teenager in a Melt Zone badge crouches next to it, running a hand along the down tube.

Reeve and Camas take off their aprons and raise a glass to the crowd.

"Wow, that line is huge," Reeve says. "How'd you do it?"

"*We* did it," Camas says. "Bear heard grumblings that the drops weren't legal. He made some calls and got his Federal Firearms License. He can take custody at the point of surrender. Guns transfer to the forge as scrap metal, not firearms."

"Bear headed that off at the pass."

"Quietly," Camas says. "Like he does everything."

Reeve laughs.

The forge is warm. Liken Torch tunes her bass clarinet in the corner. Bombardon sets the tuba on its bell.

Tilly leans into Liam, her head on his shoulder. He puts his arm around her. Aquene is asleep against his chest, her bicycle socks still on.

Across the room, Josh sits on the floor with his back against the forge wall, Eland in his lap. Camas sits beside him, her knee against his. He hands her his coffee.

Bombardon's cello notes vibrate and Liken's voice floats over conversation and laughter.

Liz finds Graeme at the edge of the crowd. She takes his hand.

He looks at her. "I'll call the island agent Monday."

She holds his hand tighter.

"But I don't ride a bicycle," Black says.

Vovo is on the forge sofa, phone to ear.

"Your gun is a golf club."

"You came," Camas says.

Del shrugs. "I was riding by."

"Surprised you own a bike."

"A bike and a gun aren't mutually exclusive."

Eland pushes between them on his balance bike. He touches Del's pedal.

"Maybe if you leave your gun at home, you can get to know your grandson."

Del looks at her. He looks down at Eland, pushes off, and coasts out of the forge.

She watches him go.

Arthur Wright finds Tilly near the side door. He has a gear bag over one shoulder and a thermos in his hand.

"Arthur!"

"I thought I'd see what you were building," he says.

"This," she says.

He looks at people picking up Melt Zone badges in the forge light. "Nice work."

"They tried to shut us down today," Tilly says.

Arthur sits. "You need a bigger name for this. This isn't just a fire anymore."

Reeve, Liam, Josh, and a handful of locals put pint glasses and coffee cups back into catering racks. Spit dances as he runs a wide broom across the forge floor.

Moore and Pedro rest together on the Barcalounger, eyes closed, Moores hand in Pedro's curls.

Ike calls out, "Cutter, seen my bike?"

CHAPTER 41

Commons Forge: Hammering the collective future into form

26.3 LBS. – 6.3 GUNS ERASED

B arry Harlan finds Camas near the back of the forge. She looks up.

"Heard you snuck some guns in under cover of the Vovo Kayak Club," Camas says.

"Brought a few more tonight."

"Right on." She wipes her hands on the rag.

Barry moves his head to the music.

"Vovo said you know Dust. Where is he anyway?"

"I don't think anyone knows."

Plinky turns the laptop toward herself. Security footage, time stamped. A woman with long dark hair on a mountain bike at the gate. A man in a neon vest.

She leans in. "Arthur Wright. Of course it is."

She clicks to the fob log. Eleven minutes. Unit 1938.

She pulls up the master inventory. Scrolls.

Unit 1938. BB Gun.

She stares at the screen.

"Damn."

She closes the laptop. Picks up her phone. Taps.

A recording:

Hello, you've reached A. Wright Precision Machining. Bicycle repairs. Still no miracles. Leave a message.

"You should've stayed retired, Arthur."

Chumbeau stands at the back of his SUV in the TRIGGER parking lot. The motorized rear liftgate rises with a chime.

Plug trots up. "Welcome back, Mr. Culvern. Can I help you?"

Plug stops, his eyes locked on the vehicle. "Where did you get that?"

Chum lifts the bicycle out. The pirate flag slaps the side of Chum's whiskered face.

CHAPTER 42

The Poof: Carries kids and groceries like a dream

28.4 LBS. – 6.9 GUNS ERASED

Parents drop off children at Sandglass Meadows School where the animals look especially fluffy and Aquene's crown is bluer today.

Tilly holds Aquene's hand and Pedro's leash. Camas has Eland on her hip.

"How did the social worker visit go?" Tilly asks.

"Barnaby came up. He's mended. So are we."

"We are."

"She cleared us for the adoption court hearing."

Tilly hugs Camas and Eland. Aquene hugs their legs.

"Arthur said the forge needs a new name. Bigger than Melt Zone."

Camas shifts Eland on her hip.

"There you go again," she says. "Turning everything into a movement."

Tilly laughs. Pedro barks.

From the porch, Headmaster Truemilk rings his bell.

Near the garden shed sits a cardboard box against the fence. Somebody has written For the Forge Art Project on the side in black marker.

Inside are toy guns collected from parents and the playground over the past month: plastic pistols, a cap gun, a silver sheriff's star with a broken barrel.

Aquene sees it.

She turns and finds Eland at the goat pen. She takes his hand and leads him across the yard.

They stop in front of the box. Aquene looks in. Eland looks in.

Aquene reaches into her jacket pocket and pulls out a Syringa wildflower. She hands it to Eland, then finds another in her other pocket.

They bend over the box, flowers in hand.

Aquene places her flower into the barrel of a plastic pistol.

She looks at Eland.

"Bullet," she says.

"Poof," he answers.

Barnaby hums.

THE END

Pedro's Primer

Tilly asked me to share a few woofs with you.

I sure loved this book. But I did not love the parts about kids and my friend Barnaby getting hurt.

Kids like to rest their foreheads in my curls. Barnaby just snorts and steals sandwiches. It makes the world go 'round.

Guns don't help the world turn.

The loud noise scares me.

My German Shorthair friend Gretel told me, "I wish my human used binoculars instead of a gun. I cry every time I bring a limp bird-friend home."

In this book alone, 212 guns were melted into 42 bicycles in the time it took you to read it—and that was in just one town.

I asked my dog AI, Scruff, how many bicycles humans could make from all the guns in the world.

You know what Scruff said?

733 million bikes.

Wow.

Or 1.9 million tiny houses. Or 220 million dog houses. That's a lot of good dogs. Or 55 million park benches where people could sit together and talk.

And there's a whole bunch of other things you can make from steel too, like wind tur-BEANS, bridges, school desks, garden tools, wheelchairs, and rain tanks. That's basically a giant bowl of water.

Sometimes I wonder if humans are afraid they won't know how to live without guns. I've done some thinking. The world is much safer when it's quiet enough to hear a sandwich wrapper opening three rooms away.

You don't need to be afraid.

P

PEDRO DE SOUSA SARAMAGO MEGELLAN

Bicycles Don't Kill

Following is a list of firearms used in some of the largest mass shootings in North America.

Note on data: Casualty counts reflect human lives lost, excluding perpetrators, and injuries directly resulting from the attacks, as reported by primary law enforcement and archival sources.[3]

Bushmaster XM15-E2S (Sandy Hook, CT — 2012) 26 Human Lives Lost. 2 Humans Injured. A civilian AR-15-style rifle. Remington marketed this model with the tagline "Consider Your Man Card Reissued," targeting younger male buyers. Families of victims sued Remington over marketing that promoted the rifle as a combat weapon, and the company later settled for $73 million.[4][5]

Glock 19 (Virginia Tech, VA — 2007) 32 Human Lives Lost. 17 Humans Injured. Originally designed for military and law enforcement use, Glock marketed its compact, high-capacity design to the civilian market, where it became one of the best-selling handguns in American history.[6][7]

Intratec TEC-9 (Columbine, CO — 1999) 13 Human Lives Lost. 21 Humans Injured. An assault pistol whose design emphasized military-style appearance and high-volume fire. Its manufacturer marketed it with language like "as tough as your toughest customer," appealing to buyers drawn to its combat look.[8] [9] [10]

Sig Sauer MCX (Orlando, FL — 2016) 49 Human Lives Lost. 53 Humans Injured. A modular rifle system marketed to civilians with an emphasis on adaptability and military association.[11]

Smith & Wesson M&P15 (Parkland, FL — 2018) 17 Human Lives Lost. 17 Humans Injured. Part of Smith & Wesson's Military and Police line, a name that borrows the credibility of professional use. It is marketed to civilians as a version of a duty-style rifle.[12]

Smith & Wesson M&P15 & DPMS Panther Arms A15 (San Bernardino, CA — 2015) 14 Human Lives Lost. 22 Humans Injured. AR-15-style rifles marketed for their affordability and tactical utility. In this domestic terror attack, the weapons were structurally modified with aftermarket components to exploit legal loopholes and bypass California's regional assault weapons restrictions.[13] [14]

Daniel Defense DDM4 V7 (Uvalde, TX — 2022) 21 Human Lives Lost. 17 Humans Injured. An AR-15 variant sold directly to consumers. According to a lawsuit, the shooter created a Daniel Defense account while still a minor, added a DDM4 V7 to his online shopping cart, and purchased the rifle shortly after turning 18.[15] [16] [17]

FN Herstal Five-seveN (Fort Hood, TX — 2009) 13 Human Lives Lost. 32 Humans Injured. Developed for military use, FN later offered a semi-automatic civilian version, emphasizing its specialized capabilities and military adoption.[18] [19]

Remington 870 (Washington Navy Yard, DC — 2013) 12 Human Lives Lost. 3 Humans Injured. A pump-action shotgun with a long history in the sporting market, later positioned within a growing tactical-defense segment.[20]

Ruger Mini-14 (École Polytechnique, Montreal, QC — 1989) 14 Human Lives Lost. 14 Humans Injured. Designed with a "ranch rifle" aesthetic to avoid the tactical appearance of AR-style weapons while retaining similar semi-automatic capabilities — a strategy that helped broaden its civilian appeal.[21] [22] [23]

Norinco Type 56 (Stockton, CA — 1989) 5 Human Lives Lost. 29 Humans Injured. A variant of the AK-47 sold on the civilian market. The 1989 schoolyard shooting of children became one of the catalysts for California's assault-weapons restrictions and later federal debate.[24] [25]

Ruger AR-556 (Sutherland Springs, TX — 2017) 26 Human Lives Lost. 20 Humans Injured. Ruger's entry-level AR-15 platform, priced and marketed for accessibility.[26]

Uzi Semi-automatic Carbine (San Ysidro, CA — 1984) 21 Human Lives Lost. 19 Humans Injured. A semi-automatic civilian version of a military submachine gun. Its compact, recognizable profile made it a natural marketing vehicle for manufacturers selling the military aesthetic to civilian buyers.[27] [28]

Remington 700 (University of Texas Tower, Austin, TX — 1966) 17 Human Lives Lost. 31 Humans Injured. A bolt-action rifle with deep roots in the hunting market. The 1966 tower shooting demonstrated the devastating reach of a precision rifle in an urban environment, and the final victim died in 2001 from a gunshot-related wound.[29] [30] [31]

Additional research sources consulted: [32] [33] [34] [35] [36] [37] [38] [39] [40]

Take Action

This book is fiction. The work is real. If you want to help reduce gun violence, support survivors, volunteer, learn more, or safely surrender firearms, these organizations are a place to begin.

Turn In or Repurpose Firearms

Support a gun turn-in or repurposing effort, donate to one, or attend a local event.

- **Guns to Gardens** (https://rawtools.org/swords-to-plow shares/) A national movement that provides a safe, legal, and community-centered way to discard unwanted firearms. Working through local networks, they host safe-surrender events where weapons are permanently disabled according to federal ATF guidelines, preventing them from ever causing future harm.

- **RAWtools** (rawtools.org) An organization dedicated to turning weapons into gardening implements, literally guiding the modern-day execution of beating swords into plowshares. They take the steel from disabled firearms and hand-forge it into tools that cultivate food, life, and community growth.

- **The Humanium Metal Initiative** (humanium-metal.com) — A global program transforming illegal firearms into peace metal for watches, pens, and art, reinvesting all proceeds into survivor support programs.

- **Art is My Weapon** (artismyweapon.org) A community initiative that takes decommissioned firearms from safe-surrender programs and distributes them to artists to create expressions of peace and healing.

- **Robby Poblete Foundation** (robbypobletefoundation.org) Founded by Pati Navalta Poblete after her son was killed by gun violence in Vallejo, California in 2014. Runs community gun buybacks and distributes decommissioned parts to artists to create works of healing and remembrance through the Art of Peace exhibition series.

- **Fonderie 47** (fonderie47.com) A global initiative that has destroyed over 70,000 AK-47s and assault rifles in Africa, transforming the metal into luxury products whose proceeds fund weapons removal programs in conflict zones.

Support Survivors and Prevention Work

Take action, volunteer, donate, organize locally, or support survivors and prevention programs through these groups. Many have targeted initiatives.

- **Everytown for Gun Safety** (everytown.org) National advocacy, research, and survivor support.

- **Sandy Hook Promise** (sandyhookpromise.org) Founded by Sandy Hook families; focused on prevention programs and youth education.

- **Brady United Against Gun Violence** (bradyunited.org) Works on legislation, litigation, and public education. Sign an open letter to Hollywood to end gun violence: https://www.bradyunited.org/take-action/join-movement /show-gun-safety/open-letter-from-hollywood-film-and-tv -leaders

- **Moms Demand Action** (momsdemandaction.org) A grassroots volunteer network active in all 50 states; part of the Everytown movement.

Learn the Facts

Read the research. Share accurate information. Support independent reporting and legal analysis.

- **Giffords Law Center** (giffords.org/lawcenter) Law center to prevent gun violence. Legal and policy analysis, including state-by-state gun law information.

- **The Trace** (thetrace.org) Independent nonprofit newsroom covering gun violence in the United States.

- **Gun Violence Archive** (gunviolencearchive.org) Real-time incident data and reporting.

Contact Your Representatives

Call, write, or meet with your elected representatives. Many advocacy organizations also provide simple online forms that help you contact your representatives in a few minutes such as Everytown.org's Action page: https://www.everytown.org/actions/

Or, write your own letter in your own words. If you use AI to help draft, here's a sample prompt:

Help me write a short, respectful message to my elected representative explaining why reducing gun violence matters to me personally. Keep it under 200 words and grounded in my own experiences and values.

- U.S. House directory (house.gov)

- Capitol switchboard (202) 224-3121

Get Crisis Support

If you or someone you love is in crisis, reach out now. Free, confidential support is available any hour of the day.

- **988 Suicide & Crisis Lifeline** (988lifeline.org) Call or text

988 for immediate support in the U.S.

- **988 Lifeline Chat** (https://chat.988lifeline.org/) Online chat is also available through the official 988 website.

If someone is in immediate danger, call 911.

Other Books by Avis Kalfsbeek

Pedro the Water Dog Saves the Planet Primers

One More Year
Plastic Plankton
Bike Rock
Copper Cobra
Planeteering
Mono Mutante

Peace Stuff Library

Peace Stuff Enough, Keep Your Stuff Longer, People *(a nonfiction companion book to One More Year on overconsumption)*

One More Year – The Hilltop Pact 10-Minute Environmental Comedy Drama *(a short performable story based on a scene from One More Year)*

Zero: The Every Person's Field Guide to a World Without Weapons

Listen & Reflect

Peace is Here Podcast with Avis Kalfsbeek

Join the Community www.AvisKalfsbeek.com

Get three FREE Prequel Short Stories

Meet the misfits before they change the world
AvisKalfsbeek.com/3free

- **Bird-Bully Besties:** See how Tilly and Camas formed their unbreakable bond back in kindergarten, long before they were pushing jogger strollers along alpine trails and standing tall on paddleboards.

- **Lucky Mustard:** Follow Ike and Bear on the Seattle docks alongside the troublemaking cat, Suerte, years before they raised the pirate flag.

- **Giro di Baci (Tour of Kisses):** Join Liz and Graeme as they cycle the Italian Alps and Tuscany, mastering the road long before Graeme found himself in Arthur Wright's precision machine shop as the world begins to shift.

These fast, funny stories are the perfect introduction to a world of friendship, mountain bike jumps, and the hopeful idea of peace.

Dirge Without Music

BY EDNA ST. VINCENT MILLAY

I am not resigned to the shutting away of loving hearts in the hard
 ground.
So it is, and so it will be, for so it has been, time out of mind:
Into the darkness they go, the wise and the lovely. Crowned
With lilies and with laurel they go; but I am not resigned.

Lovers and thinkers, into the earth with you.
Be one with the dull, the indiscriminate dust.
A fragment of what you felt, of what you knew,
A formula, a phrase remains, —but the best is lost.

The answers quick and keen, the honest look, the laughter, the love,—
They are gone. They are gone to feed the roses. Elegant and curled
Is the blossom. Fragrant is the blossom. I know. But I do not approve.
More precious was the light in your eyes than all the roses in the world.

Down, down, down into the darkness of the grave
Gently they go, the beautiful, the tender, the kind;
Quietly they go, the intelligent, the witty, the brave.
I know. But I do not approve.
And I am not resigned.

Bicycle: Elgin Bluebird, 1935–1938. Considered by many collectors to be one of the most iconic prewar American bicycles.

Endnotes

1. Berrigan, Azrael, and Miller, Annals of the American Academy of Political and Social Science, 2022

2. PeopleForBikes, 2024 Bicycling Participation Report

3. Gun Violence Archive. "Number of Deaths in 2025." Gun Violence Archive; see also Gun Violence Archive custom export of mass shooting incidents involving children, downloaded April 2026, from https://www.gunviolencearchive.org

4. WHYY. "Sandy Hook families settle for $73M with gun maker Remington." WHYY. https://whyy.org/articles/sandy-hook-families-73m-settlement-remington/

5. CBS News. "Sandy Hook families settle for $73 million with gunmaker Remington." CBS News. https://www.cbsnews.com/news/remington-sandy-hook-elementary-school-shooting-settlement-73-million/

6. Virginia Tech Review Panel. "Mass Shootings at Virginia Tech, April 16, 2007: Report of the Review Panel." https://scholar.lib.vt.edu/prevail/docs/VTReviewPanelReport.pdf

7. Violence Policy Center. "Backgrounder on Pistols Used in Virginia Tech Shooting." https://vpc.org/studies/vatechgunsbackgrounder.pdf

8. 5280 Magazine. "The Weapons of School Shooters — Columbine, 20 Years Later." https://columbine.5280.com/evolving-arsenals/

9. The Denver Post. "Columbine - Tragedy and Recovery." https://extras.denverpost.com/news/shot0423b.htm

10. Democracy Now! "TEC-9 Semi-Automatic Pistol Used in Littleton." https://www.democracynow.org/1999/4/26/tec_9_semi_automatic_pistol_used

11. The Smoking Gun. "Guns Used in the Deadliest U.S. Mass Shootings." https://smokinggun.org/guns-used-in-the-deadliest-u-s-mass-shooting/

12. Everytown for Gun Safety. "Debunking Gun Myths at the Dinner Table." https://w
ww.everytown.org/debunking-gun-myths-at-the-dinner-table/

13. 29. Federal Bureau of Investigation. "San Bernardino Shooting Investigation." https://www.fbi.gov/sanbernardino

14. 29. Los Angeles Times. "The rifles used in San Bernardino shooting were modified to
bypass California law." https://www.latimes.com/local/lanow/la-me-ln-san-bernardi-
no-shooting-guns-20151203-story.html

15. The Texas Tribune. "Uvalde families sue gun manufacturer, Instagram, Activi-
sion." https://www.texastribune.org/2024/05/24/uvalde-shooting-lawsuits-gunmak
er-instagram-texas/

16. ABC News. "Uvalde families sue makers of AR-15, 'Call of Duty,' Meta over mass
shooting." https://abcnews.com/US/uvalde-families-sue-makers-ar-15-call-duty-met
a/story?id=110548748

17. U.S. Court of Appeals for the Fourth Circuit. "Lowy v. Daniel Defense et al., No.
24-1822." https://www.ca4.uscourts.gov/opinions/241822.P.pdf

18. The White House (Obama Archives). "Public Summary of the Inventory of Files Re-
lated to Fort Hood Shooting." https://obamawhitehouse.archives.gov/the-press-offic
e/public-summary-inventory-files-related-fort-hood-shooting

19. ABC13 Houston. "Pathologist: Fort Hood victims shot numerous times." https://ab
c13.com/archive/9206261/

20. Mother Jones. "What We Do and Don't Know About the Washington Navy Yard
Mass Shooting." https://www.motherjones.com/politics/2013/09/washington-navy
-yard-mass-shooting/

21. AOAV (Action on Armed Violence). "15 shootings that changed the law: Montreal,
1989." https://aoav.org.uk/2014/montreal-1989/

22. The Globe and Mail. "Why the rifle used in the Polytechnique shooting remains legal,
30 years later." https://www.theglobeandmail.com/canada/article-ecole-polytechniq
ue-montreal-massacre-anniversary-gun-law-canada/

23. EBSCO Research Starters. "École Polytechnique massacre." https://www.ebsco.com
/research-starters/history/ecole-polytechnique-massacre

24. Sactown Magazine. "1989 Stockton School Shooting." https://www.sactownmag.com/trigger-effect/

25. Stocktonia. "In Stockton, an earlier mass shooting brought a monumental shift in gun policy." https://stocktonia.org/news/public-safety/2025/11/30/stockton-shooting-1989-assault-weapons-ban/

26. The Smoking Gun. "Guns Used in the Deadliest U.S. Mass Shootings." https://smokinggun.org/guns-used-in-the-deadliest-u-s-mass-shooting/

27. UPI Archives. "Details of McDonald killer's arsenal." https://www.upi.com/Archives/1984/07/19/Details-of-McDonald-killers-arsenal/6858459057600/

28. Violence Policy Center. "Where'd They Get Their Guns? — McDonald's Restaurant, San Ysidro, California." https://www.vpc.org/studies/wgun840718.htm

29. Texas State Historical Association. "University of Texas Tower Shooting, 1966." https://www.tshaonline.org/handbook/entries/university-of-texas-tower-shooting-1966

30. Austin Public Library. "UT Tower Shootings Resources." http://library.austintexas.gov/ahc/ut-tower-shootings-resources

31. Behind the Tower. "The Victims." http://behindthetower.org/the-victims/

32. NPR. "Families of Sandy Hook victims reach $73 million settlement with Remington." https://www.npr.org/2022/02/15/1080819088/sandy-hook-victims-families-settlement-remington

33. AP News. "Sandy Hook families settle for $73M with gun maker Remington." https://apnews.com/article/sandy-hook-school-shooting-remington-settlement-e53b95d398ee9b838afc06275a4df403

34. KHQ. "Weapons used in VA Tech shooting." https://www.khq.com/news/weapons-used-in-va-tech-shooting/article_5da43580-0490-5ba6-80ca-da240451e970.html

35. The Trace. "Gun Violence By The Numbers in 2025." https://www.thetrace.org/2025/12/data-shooting-stats-gun-violence-america/

36. Sportsmen's Alliance. "Sportsmen's Alliance Defends PLCAA in 4th Circuit Lawsuit." https://sportsmensalliance.org/news/lowy-v-daniel-defense-court-ruling-opens-door-for-lawsuits-against-firearms-manufacturers/

37. EBSCO Research Starters. "San Ysidro McDonald's massacre." https://www.ebsco.c
om/research-starters/history/san-ysidro-mcdonalds-massacre

38. Behind the Tower. "Behind the Tower: New Histories of the UT Tower Shooting."
http://behindthetower.org

39. Federal Bureau of Investigation. "San Bernardino Shooting Investigation." https://w
ww.fbi.gov/sanbernardino

40. Los Angeles Times. "The rifles used in San Bernardino shooting were modified to bypass
California law." https://www.latimes.com/local/lanow/la-me-ln-san-bernardino-sho
oting-guns-20151203-story.html

Pedro's Haiku

Guns cool into steel

Pedro noses the new frame

The child rides to school